I0634790

James Matthew Barrie

A Tillyloss Scandal

James Matthew Barrie

A Tillyloss Scandal

ISBN/EAN: 9783337408619

Printed in Europe, USA, Canada, Australia, Japan

Cover: Foto ©Andreas Hilbeck / pixelio.de

More available books at **www.hansebooks.com**

A
TILLYLOSS SCANDAL

BY

J. M. BARRIE

AUTHOR OF "THE LITTLE MINISTER," "AULD LICHT IDYLLS," "A WINDOW
IN THRUMS," ETC.

NEW YORK

LOVELL, CORYELL & COMPANY

43, 45 AND 47 EAST TENTH STREET

CONTENTS.

CONTENTS.

A TILLYLOSS SCANDAL

CHAPTER I.

IN WHICH WE APPROACH HAGGART, HAT IN HAND.

ACCORDING to those who have thought the thing over, it would defy the face of clay to set forth this prodigious affair of Tillyloss, the upshot of which was that Tammas Haggart became a humorist. It happened so far back as the Long Year, so called by reason of disease in the potato crop; and doubtless the house, which still stands, derides romance to those who cavil at an outside stair. Furthermore, the many who only knew Haggart in his later years, whether personally or through written matter or from Thrums folk who have traveled, will not readily admit that he may once have been an every-day man. There is also against me the vexing practice of the farmer of Lookaboutyou, who never passes Tillyloss, if there is a friend of mine within earshot, without saying :

"Gravestane or no gravestane, Tammas Haggart would have been a humorist."

Lookaboutyou thus implies that he knew Haggart for a man of parts when the rest of us were blind, and it is tantalizing beyond ordinary to see his word accepted in this matter by people who would not pay him for a drill of potatoes without first stepping it to make sure of the length.

I have it from Tammas Haggart that until the extraordinary incident occurred which I propose telling as he dropped it into my mouth, he was such a man as myself. True, he was occasionally persuaded by persons of Lookaboutyou's stamp to gloss over this admission, as incredible on the face of it, but that was in his last years, when he had become something of a show, and was in a puzzle about himself. Of the several reasons he gave me in proof of a non-humorous period in his life the following seem worthy of especial attention :—

First, that for some years after his marriage

he had never thought of himself as more nicely put together than other men. He could not say for certain whether he had ever thought of himself at all, his loom taking up so much of his time.

Second, that Chirsty was able to aggravate him by saying that if which was which she would have married James Pitbladdo.

Third, that he was held of little account by the neighbors, who spoke of his living " above Lunan's shoppy," but never localized the shop as "below Haggart's house."

Fourth, that while on his wanderings he experienced certain novel and singular sensations in his inside, which were probably his humor trying to force a passage.

Fifth, that in the great scene which ended his wanderings, his humor burst its banks like a dam, and had flowed in burns ever since.

During nearly forty years we contrived now and again to harness Tammas to his story, but often he would stop at the difficulty of realizing the man he must have been in his pre-humorous days, and remark, in his sarcastic way, that the one Haggart could not fathom the other. Thus our questionings sometimes ended in silence, when we all looked in trouble at the fire and then went home. As for starting him on the story when he was not in the vein, it was like breasting the brae against a high wind.

When the events happened I was only a lad. I cannot send my mind back to the time when I could pass Haggart without the side-glance nearly all Thrums offered to his reputation, and he is best pictured hunkering at Tillyloss, one of a row of his admirers. After eight o'clock it was the pleasant custom of the weavers to sit in the open against a house or dyke, their knees near their chins and their ears ready for Haggart. Then his face would be contracted in pain as some strange idea bothered him and he searched for its humorous aspect. Perhaps ten minutes afterwards his face would expand, he would slap his knees, and we knew that the struggle was over. It was one of his ways, disliked at the time, yet admired on reflection, not to take us into the secret of his laughter; but he usually ended by looking whimsically in the direction of the burying-ground, when we were perfectly aware of the source of the joke, and those of us nudged each other who were not scared. Until the spell was broken we might sit thus for the space of a quarter of an hour, none speaking, yet in the completest sympathy, because we were all thinking of the same thing, and that a gravestone.

Tillyloss is three broken rows of houses in the east end of Thrums, with gardens between them, nearly every one of which used to contain a pig-sty. There are other ways of getting into the gardens than by windows, for those who are sharp at knowing a gate when it looks like something else. Three or four other houses stand in odd corners, blocking the narrow road, which dodges through Tillyloss like a hunted animal. Starting from the west end of the suburb, as Tillyloss will be called as soon as we can say the word without smirking, the road climbs straight from the highway to the uppermost row, where it runs against a two-story house. Here we leave it, as many a curious stranger has done, to get out of Tillyloss the best way it can, for that two-storied house is where Tammas Haggart lived, up the outside stair, the west room.

Tammas flitted to the Tenements a year after he became a humorist, and it is an ex-

traordinary tribute to his memory that the
road from the pump up to his old residence in
Tillyloss is still called Haggart's Roady.
Many persons have inhabited his room since
he left it, but though the younger ones hold
out for an individuality of their own, the gray-
beards still allow that it is Haggart's house.
To this day Tillyloss residents asked for a
landmark to their dwellings may reply,

" I'm sax houses south frae Haggart's," or

" Onybody can point out Haggart's stair to
you.   Ay, weel, gang to that, and then come
back three doors."

The entrance to Lunan's shop was beneath
Haggart's stair, which provided a handy retir-
ing place in wet weather.   Lunan's personality
had the enormous advantage of a start of
Tammas's, as has been seen, yet Haggart has
practically swallowed Lunan, who in his more
crabbed age scowled at the sight-seers that
came to look at the second story of the house
and ignored the shop.   As boys we envied,
more than learning, the companion whose
father kept a shop, and I remember Lunan's son
going with his fists for the banker's son who—
though he never really believed it—said that

his father could have a shop if he liked. Yet
the grand romance of Haggart choked the
fame of Lunan even with the lads who played
dumps at Tillyloss, and the shop came to be
localized as "beneath Haggart's stair." Even
Lunan's stoutness, which was a landmark in
itself, could not save him. The passage between his counter and the wall was so narrow
and the rest of his shop so full of goods that
before customers could enter Lunan had to
come out, but in this quandary his dignity
never left him. He always declined to join
the company who might be listening on the
stair to Tammas's adventures, but some say he
was not above hearkening through a hole in
one of the steps.

The exact date of Haggart's departure cannot be determined, though it was certainly in
the back end of the year 1834. He had then
been married to Chirsty a little short of three
years. His age would be something beyond
thirty, but he never knew his birthday, and I
have heard him say that one of the few things
he could not understand was how the relatives
of a person deceased could know the precise
age to send to the newspapers.

What is, however, known for certain is that
Tammas's adventures began within a week of
the burial of old Mr. Yuill, the parish minister.
There had been a to-do about who should
preach the funeral sermon, two ministers having words over it, and all Thrums knowing
that Mr. Yuill had left seven pounds to the
preacher.   At this time Haggart did not belong
to the Auld Lichts, nor was he even regular in
his attendance at the parish church, but the
dispute about the funeral sermon interested him
greatly, and when he heard that the session
was meeting to decide the affair, he agreed with
Chirsty that he might do worse than hang
around the door on the chance of getting early
information.   There was a small crowd at the
door on the same errand, all of whom noticed,
though they little thought it would give them
a topic to their dying day, that Haggart had on
his topcoat.   It had been an old one of Mr.
Yuill's, presented to Tammas, who could not
fill it, but refused to have it altered, out of
respect to the minister's memory.   It has also
been fondly recalled of Tammas that he was
only shaven on the one side, as if Chirsty had
sent him to the meeting in a hurry, and that

he had not the look of a man who was that very night to enter upon experiences which would confound the world.

"It was an impressive spectacle," Snecky Hobart said subsequently, "to see Tammas discussing the burial sermon, just as keen as me and T'nowhead, and then to think that within twenty-four hours the very ministers themselves would be discussing him."

"He said to me it had been a dowie day," T'nowhead always remembered.

"He shoved me when he was crushing in nearer the door," was Hender Robbie's boast.

"But he took a snuff out of my mull."

"Maybe he did, but I was the last he spoke to. He said, 'Weel, Dan'l, I'll be stepping back to Tilly.'"

"Ay, but I passed him at the Tenements, and he says, 'Davit,' he says, and I says, 'Tammas.'"

"Very like ; but I was carrying a ging of water frae Susie Linn's pump, and Tammas said would I give him a drink, the which I did."

"Lads, I'm no sure but what I noticed a

far-away look in Tammas's face, as if there was something on his mind."

"If ye did, Jeames, ye kept it to yoursel'."

"Ay, but I meant to mention it when I got hame."

"How did ye no, then?"

"How does a body no do many a thing? I dinna say I noticed the look, but just that I'm no sure but what I noticed it."

So we all did our best to recall Haggart's last words and looks on that amazing evening, even the Auld Licht minister, who cared little for popularity, claiming as a noticeable thing to have walked behind Tammas and observed that his handkerchief was hanging out of his north pocket. But though all these memories have their value as relics, we have Tammas's own word for it that from the time he reached the session house until his return to Tillyloss he felt much as usual.

"Ay," he would say in his impressive way, "many a thing may happen between the aucht and the ten-o'clock bells, but I told neither T'nowhead nor Snecky nor none of them as onything was to happen that nicht."

" Ye did not, Tammas ; na, na, for if ye
had I would have heard ye, me being there."

"Ay, but ye couldna say my reason for no
telling ye ? "

" Na."

" Weel, then, my reason was just this that
I didna ken mysel'."

CHAPTER II.

CONTAINING THE CIRCUMSTANCES WHICH LED TO THE DEPARTURE OF HAGGART.

In the future Haggart's mind was to become a book in which he could turn up any page wanted, but its early stage was a ravel not worth harking back to unless for purposes of comparison. He could never, therefore, when questioned, say for certain that between the session house and Tillyloss he had met a soul except the Auld Licht minister, to see whom was naturally to feel him. At the foot of Tilly, however, he was taken aback to find a carriage and two horses standing.

The sight knocked all the news he had heard about the funeral sermon out of his head, and left him with just sufficient sense to put his back to the wall and assume the appearance of a man who would begin to think directly. First he gazed at the horses, and said,

" Ay."

Then he looked less carefully at the coach-man.

" Yes," he said.

Lastly, he gave both eyes to the carriage, and corroborated his previous remarks with,

" Umpha."

In themselves these statements suggest little, though they really left Haggart master of the situation. The first was his own answer to the question, " Will these be Balribbie's beasts ? " and the second was merely a stepping-stone to the third, which was a short way of saying that the ladies had called on Chirsty at last.

Tammas's wife, Chirsty, had been a servant at Balribbie, the mistress of which had promised, as most of Thrums was aware, to call on her some day.

" Ye'll be none the better though she does call," Haggart used to say, to which Chirsty's inhuman answer was,

" Maybe no ; but it'll make every other woman in Tillyloss miserable."

Every day for a year Chirsty awaited the coming of the ladies, after which it was the neighbors who spoke of the promised visit

rather than herself.   But evidently the ladies
had come after all, and the question for Tammas
was whether to face them or step about Tilly
until they had driven away.   It is difficult, no
doubt, to believe that there ever was a time
when Haggart would rather have hidden behind a dyke than converse with the gentry, but
I have this from himself.   He, whose greatest
topic in the future was to be, Women, and
Why we should Put up with Them, however
Unreasonable, could not think of the proper
thing to say to the ladies of Balribbie.

"Losh, losh," he has said, when casting
his mind back to this period, "it's hard to me
to believe that the unhumorous man swithering
at the foot of Tilly that nicht was really Tammas
Haggart, and no just somebody dressed up in
Tammas Haggart's image."

If it was hard to Tammas, how much harder
to the like of us.

Without actually deciding to show tail,
Tammas continued to lean heavily against the
wall, where he was not conspicuous to two
women who passed a little later with baskets on
their arms.

"I assure ye Chirsty's landed," one of

them said, " for she has her grand folk after all."

" Ay," said the other, " and Tammas is no in, so she'll no need to explain how her man's so lang and thin by what he was when she exhibited him at Balribbie."

" What do ye mean, ye limmers?" cried Haggart, stepping into sight. " I was never at Balribbie."

They slipped past him giggling, with the parting shots—

" Chirsty can tell ye what we mean," and

" And so can Jeames Pitbladdo."

Haggart probably sent his under lip over the upper one, for that was his way when troubled. He was aware that Chirsty had very nearly married Pitbladdo, but these women meant something else. Without knowing that he was doing so, he marched straight for his house, and was half-way up the outside stair when the door opened, and two ladies, accompanied by Chirsty, came out. Haggart did not even know what they were like, though he was to become such an authority on the female face and figure. He stopped, wanting the courage to go on and the discourtesy to turn back. So he merely stood politely in their way.

Chirsty gave her curls an angry shake as she saw him, but he had to be acknowledged.

" This is himsel'," she said, with the contempt a woman naturally feels for her husband.

Thus cornered, Tammas opened his mouth wide, to have his photograph taken, as it were, by the two ladies. The elder smiled and said,

" I am glad to make your acquaintance, James."

Tammas thinks she said more, but could never swear to it. To keep up with her quick way of speaking was a race for him, and at the word " James " he stumbled, as against a stone. When he came to himself,

" Thank ye, mem," he said, " but my name——"

Here Chirsty gave him a look that made him lose his words.

" Let the leddies pass, can ye no ? " she exclaimed.

For a moment Tammas did not see how they could pass, unless by returning to the house, when he could follow them and so get rid of himself. Then he had the idea of descending.

" At the same time," he said, picking up the lost words, " my name——"

"Dinna argy bargy with the leddies," said Chirsty, tripping down the stair like a lady herself, but not hoisting the color that would at that moment have best become her.

"You must come out to Balribbie again and see us, James," the elder lady remarked by way of good-night.

Tammas turned a face of appeal to his other visitor, who had been regarding him curiously.

"Do you know, James," she said, "I would not have recognized you again?"

"Very like," answered Tammas, "for ye never saw me."

"Be ashamed of yourself, James," cried Chirsty, shocked to hear husband of hers contradict a lady.

The young lady, however, only smiled.

"Oh, James," she said, playfully, "to think you have forgotten me, and I poured out your tea that day at Balribbie with my own hand."

In his after years Tammas, tempted to this extent, would have answered in some gallant words such as the young lady could have taken away with her in the carriage. But that night he was only an ordinary man.

" I never set foot in Bal——" he was reply-
ing, when Chirsty interfered.

" .Well he minds of it," she said, audaciously,
" and no farther back than Monday he says to
me, ' That was a cup of tea,' he says, ' as I
never tasted the marrows of.' "

" Wuman ! " cried Tammas.

" See to the house, James," said Chirsty,
"and I'll go as far as the carriage with the
ladies."

When Chirsty returned, five minutes afterwards, her husband was standing where she
had left him.

" My name, mem," he was saying to the
stair, "is not James, but Tammas, and it's
gospel I tell ye when I say I was never at
Balribbie in my born days."

Chirsty passed him without a word, and went
into the house, slamming the door. Tammas
and his tantrums did not seriously disturb her,
but she had been badly used on her way back
from the carriage. While helping the ladies
to their seats she had been happily conscious
of Kitty Crabb peeping at the proud sight from
the back of the doctor's dyke, and as Kitty was
the most celebrated gossip in Tillyloss, Chirsty

thought to herself, " It'll be through Tilly before bedtime."

" Ay, Kitty," she said, on her way back, looking over the dyke, " that was the Balribbie family calling on me."

Kitty, however, could never stand Chirsty's airs, and saw an opportunity of humbling her.

" I saw nobody," she answered.

" They've been in my house since half nine," cried Chirsty, anxiously, " and that was their carriage."

" I saw no carriage," sàid Kitty, cruelly.

" I saw ye gaping at it ower the dyke," Chirsty screamed, " and that's it ye hear driving east the road."

" I hear nothing," said Kitty.

" Katrine Crabb," cried Chirsty, " think shame of yourself."

" Na, Chirsty," rejoined Kitty, " ye needna blame me if your grand folk ignore ye."

So Chirsty entered her house with the dread fear that no one would give her the satisfaction of allowing that the Balribbie family had crossed its threshold. She was wringing a duster, as if it were Kitty Crabb, when Tammas stamped up the stair in no mood to offer sympathy.

He kept his bonnet on, more like a visitor than a man in his own house, but as he plumped upon a stool by the fire he flung his feet against the tongs in a way that showed he required immediate attention.

" I'm waiting," he said, after a pause.

" Take your feet off the fender," replied Chirsty.

" Tell me my name immediately," requested Tammas.

" That's what's troubling ye ? "

" It is so.   What's my name ? "

" Sal, whatever it is, I wish it wasna mine."

" Your grand folk called me James."

" So I noticed."

" How was that ? "

" Ye couldna expect the like of them to ken the ins and outs of your name."

" Nane of your tricks, wuman ; I wasna born on a Sabbath.   It was you that said my name was Jeames; ay, and what's more, ye called me Jeames yoursel'."

" Do ye think I was to conter grand folk like the Balribbie family ? "

" Conter here, conter there, I want to bottom this.   They said I had been at Balribbie."

" Weel, I think ye micht have been glad to take the credit of that."

" It's my opinion," said Tammas, " that ye've been pretending I was Jeames Pitbladdo."

" Ye micht have been proud of that, too," retorted Chirsty.

" As sure as death," said Tammas, " if ye dinna clear this up I gang to Balribbie for licht on't."

" She looked me in the face at that," Tammas used to say as he told the story, " and when she saw the michty determination in it she began to sing small. I pointed to the place whaur I wanted her to stand, and I says, ' Now, then, I'm waiting.' "

" I never pretended to ye," said Chirsty, " but what it was touch and go my no marrying Jeames Pitbladdo."

Tammas nodded.

" The leddies at Balribbie thocht it was him I was to marry."

" I daursay."

" They dinna ken about you at that time."

" They dinna seem to ken about me yet."

" Jeames used to come about Balribbie a

heap, and they saw he was after me, and Miss Mary often said to me was I fond of him? Ay, and I said he was daft about me. Then he spiered me, and after that they had him up to the house."

"So, so, and that was the time he got the tea?"

"It was so, and then I gave up my place, them promising to come and visit me when I was settled."

"Ay, but Jeames creepit off after all."

"Weel ye ken it was his superstitiousness made him give me the go-by."

"I've heard versions of the story frae folk in the toon, but I didna credit them. Ye took guid care never to tell me about it yoursel'. Ye said to me it was you that wouldna have him, no that he wouldna take you."

"He wanted me, but he was always a superstitious man, Jeames Pitbladdo. He was never fonder of me than when we parted."

"All I ken," said Tammas, "is that he wouldna buy the ring to ye, and that must either have been because he didna want ye when it came to the point, or because he was a michty greedy crittur."

" He's no greedy; and as for no caring for me, it near broke his heart to give me up. There was tears on his face when we parted."

" Havers ! what was there to keep him frae buying the ring if he wanted it ? "

" His superstitiousness."

" What is there superstitious about a ring ? "

" It wasna the ring ; it was the hiccup did it."

" Ay, I heard there was a hiccup in the story, but I didna fash about it."

" Jeames did though, and it was a very queery thing, I can tell ye, though I didna put the wecht on it that he did. As many a one kens forby me, he walked straight to Peter Lambie's shop to buy the ring, and just as he had his hand on the door he took the hiccup. Ye ken what a superstitious man Jeames is."

" If I wanted a wife it's no hiccup would stand in the road."

" Because you're ower ignorant to be super-stitious. And Jeames didna give in at the first try. He was back at the shop the next nicht, and there he took the hiccup again. Then he came to me and said in terrible disappointment as it would be wicked to marry in the face of

Providence. I never saw a man so crushed like."

" Ay, I'm no saying but what this may be true, but it doesna explain your reason for calling me Jeames."

" I call ye Tammas as a rule, when it's necessary to mention your name. Ye canna deny that."

" Tell me how I'm Jeames to the gentry."

" I wasna to disgrace mysel' to them, was I ? "

" Whaur's the disgrace in Tammas ? "

" Ye maun see, Tammas Haggart, dull as ye are, that it was a trying position for me to be in. When I left Balribbie the leddies thocht I was to marry Jeames Pitbladdo ; did they no ? "

" I daursay."

" And I had told them Jeames was complete daft about me ; and so he was, for he called his very porridge spoon after me, a thing you never did."

" Did I ever pretend to you I had these poetical ways ? "

" I wouldna have believed it, though you did. But was ever mortal woman left in sich a predicament because of a superstition ?

Nat'rally, when I married you, I didna' let on to the Balribbie family as ye wasna' Jeames Pitbladdo, and Jeames Pitbladdo they think ye to this day. What harm does it do ye?"

"Harm! It leaves me complete mixed up about mysel'. Chirsty Todd, ye have disgraced me this nicht."

Here Chirsty turned on him.

"I've disgraced ye, have I? And wha has shamed me every nicht for years, if no' yersel', Tammas Haggart?"

"In what way have I shamed ye?"

"In many a way, and particularly with what ye say at family worship. Take your feet off that fender."

"I keep my feet on the fender till I hear what new blether this is; ay, and longer if I like."

"The things ye say in the prayer is an insult."

"Canny, Chirsty Todd. That prayer, as weel ye ken, wa⸍ ⸍arned out of a book, the which was lended to me for the purpose by a flying stationer."

"Ye're a puir crittur if ye canna' make up

what to say yersel'.   Do you think you'll ever
be an elder ?   Not you."

" Wha wants to be an elder ? "

" None of your blasphemy, Tammas Haggart."

" What's wrang with the prayer ? "

" Gang through it in your head, and you'll
soon see that."

Tammas repeated the prayer aloud, but without enlightenment; whereupon Chirsty nearly
went the length of shaking him.

" Did ye not pray this minute," she said,
" ' for the heads of this house, and also the
children thereof ? ' "

" I did so."

" And have ye no' repeated these words
every nicht for near three years ? "

" And what about that ? "

" Tammas Haggart, have we any bairns ?   Is
there ' children thereof ? ' "

Tammas used to say that at this point he
took his feet off the fender.   When he spoke
it was thus—

" As sure as death, Chirsty, I never thocht
of that."

His intention was to soothe the woman, but

the utter unreasonableness of the sex, as he has pointed out, was finely illustrated by the way Chirsty took his explanation.

" Ye never thocht of it ! " she exclaimed, " Tammas, you're a most aggravating man."

In his humorous period, Haggart could have stood even this, but that night it was beyond bearing. He jumped to his feet and stumbled to the door.

" Chirsty Todd," he turned to say, slowly and emphatically, " you're a vain tid. But beware, woman, there's others than Jeames Pitbladdo as can take the hiccup."

Chirsty had strange cause to remember this prophecy, but at the moment it only sent her running to the door. Tammas was half-way down Tillyloss already, but she caught him in the back with this stone :

" Guid-nicht, Jeames ! "

With these words the Thrums Odyssey began.

CHAPTER III.

SHOWS HOW HAGGART SAT ON A DYKE LOOKING AT HIS OWN FUNERAL.

HAGGART must have left Tillyloss with Chirsty heavy on his mind, for an hour afterwards he was surprised to find himself out of Thrums. He was wandering beneath trees alongside the Whunny drain, which is said to have been chiseled from the rocks when men's wages were fourpence a day. Here he sat down, preparatory to turning back. It was now past his usual bedtime, and he had been twelve hours at work that day.

"I canna say whether I sat lang thinking about Chirsty," he afterwards admitted; "but I mind watching a water-rat running out and in among some nettles till it got mixed in my mind with the shuttle of my loom, and by that time I was likely sleeping."

The probability is that Tammas, who met no one, walked west from Tillyloss to Susie Linn's pump, where he took the back wynd and made for the drain edge by the west town end. This is the route we have usually given him—though Lookaboutyou sends him round by the den— and I have walked it often with Tammas when we were drawing up a sort of map of his wanderings. The last time I did this was in the company of William Byars, who came back to Thrums recently after nearly thirty years' absence, and spoke of Haggart the moment his eyes lighted again on Tillyloss. Those that saw him say that William was overcome with emotion when he gazed at the memorable outside stair, and at last walked away softly saying, "Haggart was a man." What I can say of my own knowledge is that William met me one day as I was coming into Thrums from my school-house and asked me as a favor to go round the "Haggart places" with him. This I mention as showing what a hold the affair we are now tracking took upon the popular mind.

I pointed out to William the very spot on which Tammas fell asleep. The drain edge path crossed the burn at that time by a footbridge of stone, and climbed a paling into the Long Parks of Auchtersmellie. A hoarding

has been erected on this bridge to make travelers go another way, but it is also as good as a
sign-post, for ten yards due south from it stands
the short thick beech against which Tammas
Haggart undoubtedly slept for nearly seven
hours on that queer night. Even Lookaboutyou admits this.

To make the scene as vivid as possible, William, at my suggestion, sat down beneath the
tree like one sleeping. I then went a little
way into the Long Parks and came back
hurriedly, making pretense that it was a dark
night. I climbed the paling, crossed the
bridge—there being two loose spars in the
hoarding—and was passing on when suddenly
I saw a man sleeping at the foot of a tree.
When regarding him I shivered, as if it was
the depth of winter, and then noted that he
had on a thick top-coat. After a little hesitation, I raised him cautiously and got the coat off
without wakening him. I was rushing off with
it when I remembered that the night was cold
for him as well as for me, and flung my old
coat down beside him. Then I hurried off, but
of course come back directly, the make-believe
being over.

Something very like this happened while Haggart was asleep, though no human eye witnessed the scene. All we are sure of is that the thief was dressed in corduroys like Tammas's, and that the coat he left behind him was a thin linen one, coarse, stained—though not torn—and apparently worthless. There were twelve buttons on it—an unusual number, but not, as Tammas discovered, too many. It is a matter for regret that this coat was not preserved.

No doubt Tammas was shivering when he woke up, but all his minor troubles were swallowed in the loss of his top-coat, which was not only a fine one, but contained every penny he had in the world, namely, seven shillings and sixpence in a linen bag. He climbed into the Long Parks looking for the thief; he ran along the drain edge looking for him, and finally he sat down in dull despair. It was a cruel loss, and now not his indignation with Chirsty, but Chirsty's case against him, shook his frame.

"The first use I ever made of the linen coat," he allowed, "was to wipe the water off my een wi't."

Only fear of Chirsty can explain Haggart's next step, which was, after putting on the linen coat, to wander off by the Long Parks, instead of at once returning to Tillyloss.

I did not take William over the ground covered by Haggart during the next three days; indeed, the great part of it is only known to me by vague report. Tammas doubtless had no notion when he ran away, as one might call it, from Chirsty, that he would sleep next night thirty miles from Thrums. At the back of the house of Auchtersmellie, however, he fell in with a wandering tailor, bound for a glen farm, where six weeks' work awaited him. He was not a man of these parts, but Tammas offered to walk a few miles with him, and ended by going the whole way. Of Haggart's experiences at this time I know much, but none of them is visible beside the surprising event that sent him homewards striding.

It takes one aback to think that Haggart might never have been a humorist had not one of the buttons fallen off his coat. The immediate effect of this was dramatic rather than humorous. The tailor picked up the button to sew it on to the coat again, but surprised by its weight had the curiosity to tear its linen covering with his scissors. Then he drew in his breath, extending his eyes and looking so like a man who would presently whistle with surprise that Haggart stooped forward to regard the button closely. Next moment he had snatched up the button with one hand and the coat with another, and was off like a racer to the tinkle of the starter's bell.

When beyond pursuit, Haggart sat down to make certain that he was really a rich man. The button that had fallen off was a guinea— gold guineas we said in Thrums, out of respect for them—covered with cloth, and a brief examination showed that the eleven other buttons were of the same costly kind. One popular explanation of this mysterious affair is that the tramp who left this coat to Tammas had stolen it from some person unknown, without realizing its value. Who the owner was has never been discovered, but he was doubtless a miser, who liked to carry his hoard about with him unostentatiously. I have known of larger sums hidden by farmers in as unlikely places.

Before resuming his triumphal march home, Tammas pricked a hole in each of the buttons, to make sure of his fortune, and wasted some time in deciding that it would be safer to carry the guineas as they were than stowed away in his boots.

" Sometimes on the road home," he used to say, " I ran my head on a tree or splashed into a bog, for it's sair work to keep your een on twelve buttons when they're all in different places. Lads, I watched them as if they were living things."

William and I crossed from the drain edge to the hill, where the next scene in the drama was played. The hill is public ground to the north of Thrums, separated from it by the cemetery and a few fields. So steep is the descent that a heavy stone pushed from the south side of the hill-dyke might crash two minutes afterwards against the back walls of Tillyloss. The view from the hill is among the most extensive in Scotland, and it also exposes some dilapidated courts in Thrums that are difficult to find when you are within a few feet of them. Fifty years ago the hill was nearly covered with whins, and it is half hidden in them still, despite the life-work of D. Fittis.

For some reason that I probably never knew, we always called him D. Fittis, but tradition

remembers him as the Whinslayer. At a time
when neither William nor I was of an age to
play smuggle, D. Fittis's wife lay dying far up
Glen Quharity. Her head was on D. Fittis's
breast, and the tears on her cheeks came from
his eyes. There were no human beings within
an hour's trudge of them, and what made D.
Fittis gulp was that he must leave Betsy alone
while he ran through the long night for the
Thrums doctor, or sit with her till she
died.

" Ye'll no leave me, Davie," she said.

"Oh, Betsy ; if I had the doctor, ye micht
live."

Betsy did not think she could live, but she
knew her man writhed in his helplessness, and
she told him to go.

" Put on your cravat, Davie," she said, " and
mind and button up your coat."

. " Oh, but I'm loth to gang frae ye," he said
when his cravat was round his neck and he
stood holding Betsy's hand.

" God's with me, Davie, and with you,"
Betsy said, but she could not help clinging to
him, and then D. Fittis cried, " Oh, blessed God,
Thou who didst in Thy great wisdom make

poor folk like me, in Thy hands I leave this woman, and oh, ye micht spare her to me."

"Ay, but God's will be done," said Betsy. "He kens best."

It was not God's will that these two should meet again on this earth. At the school-house, which was to become my home, D. Fittis found friends who hastened to his wife's side, and Craigiebuckle lent him a horse on which he galloped off to Thrums. But among the whins of the hill the horse flung him and broke his leg. D. Fittis tried to crawl the rest of the way, but he was found next morning in a wild state among the whins, and he was never a sane man again. For the remainder of his life he had but one passion—to cut down the whins, and many a time, at early morn, at noon, and when gloaming was coming on, I have seen him busy among them with his scythe. They grew as fast as he could cut, but he had loving relatives to tend him, and was still a kindly harmless man, though his laugh was empty.

William and I waded through the whins to a hollow in the hill, known as the toad's hole. It was here that Haggart, returning boldly to

Thrums four days after Chirsty had the last word, fell in with D. Fittis.

" He was cutting away at the whins," Tammas remembered, " and I dinna think that the whole time me and him spoke he ever raised his head; he was a terrible busy man, D. Fittis."

Haggart, big with his buttons, had, doubtless, as he approached the whinslayer, the bosom of a victorious soldier marching home to music. Nevertheless it has been noticed that the warrior, who thrives on battles, may, even in the hour of his greatest glory, be forever laid prone by a chimney can. For Tammas Haggart, confident that a few minutes would see him in Tillyloss, was preparing a surprise that rooted him to the toad's-hole like a whin. I have a poor memory if I cannot remember Haggart's own words on this matter.

"I stood looking at D. Fittis for a while," he told me, " but I said nothing loud out, though the chances are I was pitying the stocky in my mind. Then I says to him in an ordinary voice, not expecting a dumfounding answer, I says, ' Ay, D. Fittis, and is there onything fresh in Thrums?'

" He hacks away at the whins, but says he,
' The bural's this day.'

" ' Man,' I says, ' so there's a funeral!
Wha's dead?'

" ' Ye ken fine,' says he, implying as the
thing was notorious.

" ' Na,' I says, ' I dinna ken. Wha is it?'

" ' Weel,' says he, ' it's Tammas Haggart.' "

Tammas always warned us here against
attempting to realize his feelings at these mon-
strous words. " I dinna say I can picture my
position now mysel'," he said, " but one thing
sure is that for the moment these buttons
slipped clean out of my head. It was an eerie-
like thing to see D. Fittis cutting away at the
whins after making such an announcement. A
common death couldna have affected him
less."

" ' Say wha's dead again, D. Fittis,' I cries,
minding that the body was daft.

" ' Tammas Haggart,' says he, with the ut-
most confidence.

" ' Man, D. Fittis,' I says, with uncontrolled
indignation, ' ye're a big liar.'

" ' Whaever ye are,' says he, ' I would lick
ye for saying that if I could spare the time.'

" ' Whaever I am ! ' I cries. ' Very weel ye ken I'm Tammas Haggart.'

" ' Wha's the liar now ? ' says he.

" I was a sort of staggered at this, and I says sharp-like, ' What did Tammas Haggart die of ? '

" I thocht that would puzzle him, if it was just his daftness that made him say I was gone, but he had his cause of death ready. ' He fell down the quarry,' says he.

" Weel, lads, his confidence about the thing sickened me, and I says, ' Leave these whins alone, D. Fittis, and tell me all about it. '

" ' I canna stop my work,' he says, ' but Tammas Haggart fell down the 'quarry four nichts since. Ou, it was in the middle of the nicht, and all Thrums were sleeping when it was wakeued by one awful scream. It wakened the whole town. Ay, a heap of folk set up sudden in their beds.'

" ' And was that Tammas Haggart falling down the quarry ? ' I says, earnest-like, for I was a kind of awestruck.

" ' It was so,' says he, tearing away in the whins.

" ' They didna find the body, though,' I says, looking down on mysel' with satisfaction.

" ' Ay,' says he, ' the masons found it the next morning, and there was a richt rush of folk to see it.'

" ' Ye had been there ? ' I says.

" ' I was,' says he, ' and so was the wifie as lives beneath me. She took her bairn too,- for she said, " It'll be something for the little ane to boast about having seen when he grows bigger." Ay, man, it had been a michty fall, and the face wasna recognizable.'

" ' How did they ken, then,' says I, ' that it was Tammas Haggart ? '

" ' Ou,' says he at once, ' they kent him by his top-coat.'

" Lads, of course I saw in a klink that the man as stole my top-coat had fallen down the quarry and been mista'en for me. Weel, I nipped mysel' at that. It's an unco thing to say, but I admit I was glad to have this proof, as ye may call it, that it was really me as was standing in the toad's hole.

" ' When did ye say the bural was ? ' I asked him.

" ' It's at half three this day,' he says, ' and I'll warrant it's half three now, so if ye want to be sure ye're no Tammas Haggart ye can see him buried.'

"I took a long look at D. Fittis, and it's gospel I tell ye when I say I never liked him from that minute. Then I hurried up the hill to the cemetery dyke, and sat down on it. Lads, I sat there, just at the very corner, whaur they've since put a cross to mark the spot, and I watched my ain bural. Yes, there I sat for near an hour, me, Tammas Haggart, an ordinary man at that time, getting sich an experience as has been denied to the most highly edicated in the land. I'm no boasting, but facts is facts.

"I'm no saying it wasna a fearsome sight, for I had a terrible sinking at the heart, and a mortal terror took grip of me, so that I couldna have got off that dyke except by falling. Ay, and when the grave was filled up and the mourners had dribbled away, I sat on with some uncommon thochts in my mind. It would be wearing on to four o'clock when I got up shivering, and walked back to whaur D. Fittis was working. There was a question I wanted to put to him.

"'D. Fittis,' I says, 'was there ony of the Balribbie folk as visited Tammas Haggart's wife in her affliction?'

"'Ay,' says the crittur, trying to break a supple whin with his foot, 'the wifie as lives beneath me was in the house at Tillyloss when in walks a grand leddy.'

"'So, so,' I says, 'and was Chirsty ta'en up like about her man being dead?'

"'Ay,' says D. Fittis, 'she was greeting, but as soon as the grand woman comes in, Chirsty takes the wifie as lives beneath me into a corner and whispers to her.'

"'D. Fittis,' I says, sternly, 'tell me what Chirsty Todd whispered, for muckle depends on it.'

"Weel,' he says, 'she whispered, "If the leddy calls the corpse 'Jeames' dinna conterdict her."'

"I denounced Chirsty in my heart at that, not being sufficient of a humorist to make allowance for women, and I says, just to see if the thing was commonly kent, I says,

"' And wha would Jeames be?'

"'I dinna ken,' says D. Fittis, 'but maybe you're Jeames yersel', when ye canna be Tammas Haggart.'

"Lads, ye see now that it was D. Fittis as put it into my head to do what I subsequently did. 'Jeames,' I said, 'I'll be frae this hour,' and without another word I walked off in the opposite direction frae Thrums.

"I dinna pretend as it was Chirsty's behavior alone that sent me wandering through the land. I had a dread of that funeral for one thing, and for another I had twelve gold guineas about me. Moreover, the ambition to travel took hold of me, and I thocht Chirsty's worst trials was over at ony rate, and that she was used to my being dead now."

"But the well-wisher, Tammas?" we would say at this stage.

"Ay, I'm coming to that. I walked at a michty stride alang the hill and round by the road at the back of the three-cornered wood to near as far as the farm of Glassal, and there I sat down at the roadside. I was beginning to be mair anxious about Chirsty now, and to think I was fell fond of her for all her exasperating ways. I was torn with conflicting emotions, of which the one said, 'Back ye go to Tillyloss,' but the other says, 'Ye'll never have a chance like this again.' Weel, I could not persuade mysel', though I did my best, to gang back to my loom and hand ower the siller to Chirsty, and so, as ye all ken, I compromised. I hurried back to the hill——"

" But ye've forgotten the cheese ? "

" Na, listen : I hurried back to the hill, wondering how I could send a guinea to Chirsty, and I minded that I had about half a pound of cheese in my pouch, the which I had got at a farm in Glen Quharity. Weel, I shoved a guinea into the cheese, and back I goes to the hill to D. Fittis.

" 'D. Fittis,' I says, ' I ken you're an honest man, and I want ye to take this bit of cheese to Chirsty Todd.'

" ' Ay,' he says, ' I'll take it, but no till it's ower dark for me to see the whins.'

" What a busy crittur D. Fittis was, and to no end ! I left the cheese with him, and was off again, when he cries me back.

" ' Wha will I say sent the cheese ? ' he asks. I considered a minute, and then I says, ' Tell her,' I says, ' that it is frae a well-wisher.'

" These were my last words to D. Fittis, for I was feared other folk micht see me, and away I ran. Yes, lads, I covered twenty miles that day, never stopping till I got to Dundee."

It was Haggart's way, when he told his

story, to pause now and again for comments, and this was a point where we all wagged our heads, the question being whether his assumption of the character of a well-wisher was not a clear proof of humor. "That there was humor in it," Haggart would say, when summing up, "I can now see, but compared to what was to follow, it was neither here nor there. My humor at that time was like a laddie trying to open a stiff gate, and even when it did squeeze past, the gate closed again with a snap. Ay, lads, just listen, and ye'll hear how it came about as the gate opened wide, never to close again."

"Ye had the stuff in ye, though," Lookaboutyou would say, "and therefore, I'm of opinion that ye've been a humorist frae the cradle."

"Little you ken about it," Haggart would answer. "No doubt I had the material of humor in me, but it was raw. I'm thinking cold water and kail and carrots and a penny bone are the materials broth is made of?"

"They are, they are."

"Ay, but it's no broth till it boils?"

"So it's no. Ye're richt, Tammas."

4

"Weel, then, it's the same with humor. Considering me as a humorist, ye micht say that when my travels began I had put mysel' on the fire to boil."

CHAPTER IV.

THE WANDERINGS OF HAGGART.

NOT having a Haggart head on my shoulders I dare not attempt to follow the explorer step by step during his wanderings of the next five months. In that time he journeyed through at least one country, unconsciously absorbing everything that his conjurer's wand could turn to humor when the knack came to him. This admission he has himself signed in conversation.

" Ay," he said, " I was like a blind beggar in these days, and the dog that led me by a string was my impulses."

Most of us let this pass, with the reflection that Haggart could not have said it in his pre-humorous days, but Snecky Hobart put in his word.

" Ye were hardly like the blind beggar,"

he said, "for ye didna carry a tanker for folk
to put bawbees in."

Snecky explained afterwards that he only
spoke to give Haggart an opportunity. It
was, indeed, the way of all of us, when we
saw an opening, to coax Tammas into it. So
sportsmen of another kind can point out the
hare to their dogs, and confidently await
results.

"Ye're wrang, Snecky," replied Haggart.

As ever, before shooting his bolt, he then
paused. His mouth was open, and he had
the appearance of a man hearkening intensely
for some communication from below. There
were those who went the length of hinting
that on these occasions something inside
jumped to his mouth and told him what to
say.

"Yes, Snecky," he said at last, "ye're
wrang. My mouth was the tanker, and the
folk I met had all to pay toll, as ye may say,
for they dropped things into my mouth that
my humor turns to as muckle account as
though they were bawbees. I'm no sure——"

"There's no many things ye're no sure of,
Tammas."

" And this is no one of them. It's just a form of expression, and if ye interrupt me again, Snecky Hobart, I'll say a sarcastic thing about you that instant. What I was to say was that I'm no sure but what a humorist swallows everybody whole that he falls in with."

The impossibility of telling everything that befell Haggart in his wanderings is best proved in his own words:

" My adventures," he said, " was so surprising thick that when I cast them over in my mind I'm like a man in a corn-field, and every stalk of corn an adventure. Lads, it's useless to expect me to give you the history of ilka stalk. I wrax out my left hand, and I grip something, namely, an adventure; or I wrax out my right hand and grip something, namely, another adventure. Well, by keeping straight on in ony direction we wade through adventures till we get out of the field, that is to say, till we land back at Thrums. Ye say my adventures sounds different on different nichts. Precisely, for it all depends on which direction I splash off in."

Without going the length of saying that

Haggart splashed more than was necessary, I may perhaps express regret that he never saw his way to clearing up certain disputed passages in his wanderings. I would, I know, be ill-thought of among the friends who survive him if I stated for a fact that he never reached London. There was a general wish that he should have taken London in his travels, and if Haggart had a weakness it was his reluctance to disappoint an audience. I must own that he trod down his corn-field pretty thoroughly before his hand touched the corn-stalk called London, and that his London reminiscences never seemed to me to have quite the air of reality that filled his recollections of Edinburgh. Admitted that he confirmed glibly as an eye-witness the report that London houses have no gardens (except at the back), it remains undoubted that Craigiebuckle confused him with the question :—

" What do they charge in London for half-a-pound of boiling beef and a penny bone ? "

Haggart answered, but after a pause, as if he had forgotten the price, which scarcely seems natural. However, I do not say that he was never in London, and certainly his curious adventures in it are still retailed, especially one with an ignorant policeman who could not tell him which was the road to Thrums, and another with the doorkeeper of the House of Parliament, who, on being asked by Haggart " How much was to pay ? " foolishly answered " What you please."

But though I heartily approve the feeling in Thrums against those carping critics who would slice bits ' off the statue which we may be said to have reared to Haggart's memory, some of the stories now fondly cherished are undoubtedly mythical. For instance, whatever Lookaboutyou may say, I do not believe that Haggart once flung a clod of earth at the Pope. It is perfectly true that some such story got abroad, but if countenanced by Haggart it was only because Chirsty had her own reasons for wanting him to stand well with the Auld Licht minister. Often Haggart was said in his own presence to have had adventures in such places as were suddenly discovered by us in the newspapers, places that had acquired a public interest, say, because of a murder ; and then he neither agreed that he had been there nor allowed that he had not. Thus

it is reasonable to believe that his less discrim-
inating admirers splashed out of Haggart's
corn-field into some other body's without notic-
ing that they had crossed the dyke.   His silence
at those times is a little aggravating to his
chronicler now, but I would be the first to
defend it against detractors.   Unquestionably
the length of time during which Haggart
would put his under lip over the upper one,
and so shut the door on words, was one of the
grandest proofs of his humor.   However
plentiful the water in the dam may be, there
are occasions when it is handy to let down the
sluice.

I the more readily grant that certain of the
Haggart stories may have been plucked from
the wrong fields, because there still remain a
sufficient number of authenticated ones to fill
the mind with rapture.   A statistician could
tell how far they would reach round the world,
supposing they were represented by a brick
apiece, or how long they would take to pass
through a doorway on each other's heels.   We
never attempted to count them.   Being only
average men we could not conveniently carry
beyond a certain number of the stories about

with us, and thus many would doubtless now
be lost were it not that some of us loaded
ourselves with one lot and others with another.
Each had his favorites, and Haggart sup-
plied us with the article we wanted, just as
if he and we were on opposite sides of a
counter. Thus when we discuss him now we
may have new things to tell of him; nay,
even the descendants of his friends are worth
listening to on Haggart, for the stories have
been passed on from father to son.

Some enjoyed most his reminiscences of how
he felt each time he had to cut off another
button.

"Lads," he said, "I wasna unlike a doctor.
Ye mind Doctor Skene saying as how the
young doctors at the college grew faint like at
first when they saw blood gushing, but by
and by they became so michty hardy that they
could off with a leg as cool as though they
were just hacking sticks?"

"Ay, he said that."

"Weel, that was my sensations. When I
cut off the first button it was like sticking the
knife into mysel', and I did it in the dark because I hadna the heart to look on. Ay, the

next button was a stiff job too, but after that
I grew what ye may call hard-hearted, and it's
scarce going beyond the truth to say that a
time came when I had a positive pleasure in
sending the siller flying. I dinna ken, thinking the thing out calmly now, but what I was
like a wild beast drunk with blood."

"What was the most ye ever spent in a
week?"

"I could tell ye that, but I would rather ye
wanted to ken what was the most I ever spent
in a nicht."

"How muckle?'

"Try a guess."

"Twa shillings?

"Twa shillings!" cried Haggart, with a
contempt that would have been severe had the
coins been pennies; "ay, sax shillings is
nearer the mark."

"In one nicht?"

"Ay, in one single nicht."

"Ye must have lost some of it?"

"Not a bawbee. Ah, T'nowhead, man, ye
little ken how the money goes in grand towns.
Them as lives like lords must spend like lords."

"That's reasonable enough, but I would

like to hear the price of ilka thing ye got that nicht?"

" And I could tell ye. What do ye say to a shilling and saxpence for a bed?"

"I say it was an intake."

"Of course it was, but I didna grudge it."

" Ye didna?"

"No, I didna. It was in Edinburgh, and my last nicht in the place, and also my last button, so I thinks to mysel' I'll have one tremendous, memorable nicht, and then I'll go hame. Lads, I was a sort of wearying for Chirsty."

" Ay, but there's four shillings and saxpence to account for yet."

" There is so. Saxpence of it goes for a glass of whisky in the smoking-room. Lads, that smoking-room was a sight utterly baffling imagination. There was no chairs in it except great muckle saft ones, a hantle safter than a chaff bed, and in ilka chair some nobleman or other with his feet up in the air. Ay, I a sort of slipped the first time I tried a chair, but I wasna to be beat, for thinks I, ' Lords ye may be, but I have paid one and sax for my bed as weel as you, and this nicht I'll be a lord too!'　Keeping the one and sax before me made me bold, and soon I was sprawling in a chair with my legs sticking ower the arm with the best of them.　Ay, it wasna so much enjoyable as awe-inspiring."

" That just brings ye up to twa shillings."

" Weel, there was another one and sax for breakfast."

" Astounding!"

" Oh, a haver, of course, but we got as muckle as we liked, and I assure ye it's amazing how much ye can eat, when ye ken ye have to pay for it at ony rate.　Then there was ninepence for a luncheon."

" What's that?"

" I didna ken mysel' when I heard them speaking about it, but it turned out to be a grand name for a rabbit."

" Man, is there rabbits in Edinburgh?"

" Next there was threepence of a present to the waiter-loon, and I finished up with a shilling's worth of sangwiches."

" Na, that's just five and saxpence."

Haggart, however, would not always tell how the remaining sixpence went.　At first he admitted having squandered it on the theatre, but after he was landed by Chirsty in the Auld Licht kirk he withdrew this reminiscence, and put another sixpence-worth in the smoking-room in its place.

As a convincing proof of the size of Edinburgh, Haggart could tell us how he lost his first lodgings in it. They were next house to a shop which had a great show of vegetables on a board at the door, and Haggart trusted to this shop as a landmark. When he returned to the street, however, there were greengrocery shops everywhere, and after asking at a number of doors if it was here he lived, he gave up the search. This experience has been paralleled in later days by a Tilliedrum minister, who went for a holiday to London, and forgot the name of the hotel he was staying at; so he telegraphed to Tilliedrum to his wife, asking her to tell him what address he had given her when he wrote, and she telegraphed back to him to come home at once.

Like all the great towns Haggart visited, Edinburgh proved to be running with low characters, with whom, as well as with the flower of the place—for he was received everywhere—he had many strange adventures. His

affair with the bailie would make a long story
itself, if told in full as he told it; also what he
did to the piper; how he climbed up the
Castle rocks for a wager; why he once marched
indignantly out of a church in the middle of
the singing; the circumstances in which he
cut off his sixth button; his heroic defense of
a lady who had been attacked by a footpad;
his adventures with the soldier who was in
love and had a silver snuffbox; his odd meeting
with James Stewart, lawful King of Great
Britain and Ireland. With this personage,
between whom and a throne there only stood
the constables, Haggart of Thrums hobnobbed
on equal terms. The way they met was this.
Haggart was desirous of the sensation of
driving in a carriage, but grudged much out-
lay on an experience that would soon be over.
He accordingly opened the door of a street
vehicle and stepped in, when the driver was
not looking. They had a pleasant drive along
famous Princes Street and would probably have
gone farther had not Haggart become aware
that someone was hanging on behind. In his
indignation he called the driver's attention
to this, which led to his own eviction. The

hanger-on proved to be no other than the hapless monarch, with whom Haggart subsequently broke a button. For a king, James Stewart, who disguised his royal person in corduroys, was, as Haggart allowed, very ill in order. The spite of the authorities had crushed that once proud spirit, and darkened his intellect, and he took his friend to a gambling-house, where he nodded to the proprietor.

" Whether they were in company, with designs on my buttons," Haggart has said, " I'm not in a position to say, but I bear no ill-will to them. They treated me most honorable. Ay, the king, as we may call him if we speak in a low voice, advises me strong to gamble a button at one go, for, says he, ' You're sure to win.' Lads, it's no for me to say a word against him, but I thocht I saw him wink to the proprietor lad, and so I says in a loud voice, says I, ' I'll gamble half-a-crown first, and if I win, then I'll put down a button.' The proprietor a sort of nods to the king at that, and I plunks down my half-crown. Weel, lads I won five shillings in a clink."

" Ay, but they were just waiting for your guinea."

"It may have been so, Andrew, but we have no proof of that; for, ye see, as soon as I got the five shillings and had buttoned it up in my pouch, I says, 'I'll be stepping hame now,' I says, and away I goes. Ye canna say but what they treated me honorable."

"They had looked thrawn?"

"Ou, they did; but a man's face is his own to twist it as he pleases."

"And ye never saw the king again?"

"Ay, I met him after that in a close. I gave the aristocratic crittur saxpence."

"I'll tell ye what, Tammas Haggart: if he was proclaimed king, he would very likely send for ye to the palace and make ye a knight."

"Man, Snecky, I put him through his catechism on that very subject, but he had no hope. Ye canna think how complete despondent he was."

"Ye're sure he was a genuine Pretender?"

"Na faags! But when ye're traveling it doesna do to let on what ye think, and I own it's a kind of satisfaction to me now to picture mysel' diddling a king out of five shillings."

"It's a satisfaction to everybody in Thrums, Tammas, and more particular to Tillyloss."

" Ay, Tilly has the credit of it in a manner of speaking. And it was just touch and go that I didna do a thing with the siller as would have commemorated that adventure among future ages."

" Ay, man ? "

" I had the notion to get bawbees for the money, namely, one hundred and thirty-twa bawbees, for of course I didna count the saxpence. Well, what was I to do with them ? "

" Put the whole lot in the kirk-plate the first Sabbath day after ye came back to Thrums? "

" Na, na. My idea was to present a bawbee to a hundred and thirty-twa folk in Thrums, so as they could keep it round their necks or in a drawer as a memento of one of their humble fellow-townsmen."

" No humble, surely ? "

" Maybe no, but when ye do a thing in a big public way it's the proper custom to speak of yersel' as a puir crittur, and leave the other speakers to tell the truth about ye."

" It's a pity ye didna carry out that notion."

" Na, it's no, for I had a better ane after, the which I did carry out."

" Yea? "

"Ay, I bocht a broach to Chirsty with the siller."

"Ho, ho, that's whaur she got the broach?"

"It is so, and though I dinna want to boast, nobody having less need to do so, I can tell ye it was the biggest broach in Edinburgh at the price."

Edinburgh was only a corner in Haggart's field of corn, and from it I have not pulled half-a-dozen stalks. He was in various other great centers of adventure, and even in wandering between them he had experiences such as would have been a load for any ordinary man's back. Once he turned showman, when the actors were paid in the pennies flung at them by admirers in the audience. Haggart made for himself a long blood-red nose, which proved such an irresistible target for moneyed sportsmen that the other players complained to the management. He sailed up canals swarming with monsters of the deep. He proved such an agreeable companion at farms that sometimes he had to escape in the night. He rescued a child from drowning and cowed a tiger by the power of the human eye, exactly as these things are done in a book which belonged to Chirsty. He had eleven guineas with him when he set out, and without a note-book he could tell how every penny of the money was spent. Prices, indeed, he remembered better than anything.

I might as well attempt to walk up the wall of a house as to cut my way through Haggart's corn-field. Before arriving at the field I thought to get through it by taking the buttons one by one, but here I am at the end of a chapter, and scarcely any of the corn is behind me. I now see that no biographer will ever be able to treat Haggart on the grand scale he demands; for humility will force those who knew him in his prime to draw back scared from the attempt, while younger admirers have not the shadow of his personality to warn them of their responsibility. For my own part, I publicly back out of the field, and sit down on the doctor's dyke awaiting Haggart's return to Thrums.

CHAPTER V.

THE RETURN OF HAGGART.

HAGGART came home on a Saturday evening, when the water-barrels were running over, and our muddy roads had lost their grip. But at all times he took small note of the weather, and often said it was a fine day out of politeness to the acquaintances he met casually, when Tillyloss dripped in rain. To a man who has his loom for master it only occurs as an afterthought to look out at the window.

His shortest and natural route would have taken the wanderer to Tillyloss without zigzagging him through the rest of Thrums, but he made a circuit of the town, and came marching down the Roods.

"I wanted to burst upon the place sudden like," he admitted, "and to let everybody see me. I dinna deny but what it was a proud moment, lads, as Thrums came in sicht. I had naturally a sort of contempt for the placey, and yet I was fell awid to be back in it too, just as a body is glad to slip into his bed at nicht. Ay, foreign parts is grand for adventure, but Thrums for company."

At the top of the Roods he was recognized by two boys who had been to a farm for milk, and were playing at swinging their flagon over their heads without dropping its contents. The apparition stayed the flagon in the air, and the boys clattered off screaming. Their father had subsequently high words with Tammas, who refused to refund the price of the milk.

" Though my expectations was high," Haggart said, " they were completely beaten by the reality. Nothing could have been more gratifying than the sensation I created, not only among laddies and lassies but among grown men and women. Very weel I ken that Dan'l Strachen pretends he stood his ground when I came upon him at the mouth of Saunders Rae's close, but whaur was the honor in that, when the crittur was paralyzed with fear ? Ay, he wasna the only man that

lost his legs in the Roods that day; Will'um
Crewe being another. Snecky Hobart, you
was one of them as I walked into at Peter
Lambie's shop door, and I'll never speak to ye
again if ye dinna allow as I scattered ye like a
showman in the square does when he passes
round the hat."

"I allow, Tammas, as I made my feet my
friend that nicht."

"And did I no send the women flying and
skirling in all directions? Was it me or was
it no me that made Mysy Dinnie faint on her
back in the corner of the school-wynd?"

"It was you, Tammas, and michty boastful
the crittur was when she came to, and heard
she had fainted."

"And there's a curran women as says they
hung out at their windows looking at me. I
would like to hear of one proved case in which
ony woman did that except at a second story
window?

"Sal, they didna dare look out at low windows. Na, they were more like putting on
their shutters.

"And did some of them no bar their doors,
and am I lying when I say Lisbeth Whamand

up with her bairn out of the cradle and ran to
the door of the Auld Licht kirk, thinking I
couldna harm her there ? "

" You're speaking gospel, Tammas. And
it wasna to be wondered at that we should be
terrified, seeing we had buried ye five months
before."

" I'm no saying it was unnatural. I would
have been particular annoyed if ye had been
so stupid as to stand your ground. And what's
more, if I had met the Auld Licht minister he
would have run like the rest."

But this oft-repeated assertion of Haggart's
was usually received in silence. His extraordinary imagination enabled him to conceive
this picture, but to such a height we never
rose.

By the time Haggart reached the Tenements
the town had sufficiently recovered to follow
him at a distance. How he looked to the populace has been frequently discussed, Peter
Lambie's description being regarded as the
best.

" Them of you," Peter would say, drawn to
the door of his shop by Haggart groups, " as
has been to the Glen Quharity Hieland sports,

can call to mind the competition for best-dressed Hielander. The Hielanders stands in their glory in a row, and the grand leddies picks out the best-dressed one. Weel, the competitors tries to look as if they didna ken they were being admired, implying as they're indifferent to whether they get the prize or no, but, all the time, there's a sort of pleased smirk on their faces, mixed up with a natural anxiety. Ay, then, that's the look Tammas Haggart had when he passed my shop."

" But ye saw a change come ower him, did ye no ? "

" I did. I was among them as ran after him along the Tenements, and, though I just saw his back, it wasna the back he had on when he passed my shop. I would say, judging from his back, as his chest was sticking out, and he walked with a sort of strut, like the Hielander as has won the prize and kens it would be a haver to make pretence of modesty ony more."

" But ye never saw me look back, Pete," Haggart said, when Lambie's version was presented to him.

" Na, it was astonishing how he could have

kept frae turning your head. Ye was like one unaware that there was sich a crowd running after ye."

" Ay, lad, but very weel I kent for all that. Thinks I to mysel' as I walks on before ye— ' This scene winna be forgotten for many a year.' "

" And it will not, Tammas. It did the work of the town for a nine days. Ay, I've often said myself that you walked hame that nicht more like a circus procession than a single man. The only thing I a kind of shake my head at is your saying ye wasna a humorist at that time."

" I didna just gang that length, Pete. I was a humorist and I wasna a humorist. My humor was just peeping out of its hole like a rabbit, as ye micht say."

" Ye said as when ye started on your wanderings it was like putting yoursel', considered as a humorist, on the fire to boil. Weel, then, I say as ye had come aboil when ye marched through Thrums."

" Na, Lookaboutyou, it's an ingenious argument that; but ye've shot ower the top of the target, lad. Ye've all seen water so terrible near the boil that if ye touch it with your finger it does begin to boil?"

"Ay, that's true; but a spoon is better to touch it with, in case you burn your finger."

Lookaboutyou got a laugh for this, which annoyed Tammas.

"Take care, Lookaboutyou," he said, warningly, "or I'll let ye see as my humor can burn too. I ken a sarcastic thing to say to ye, my man."

"But what about the water so near the boil?" asked Hobart, while Lookaboutyou shrunk back.

"My humor was in that condition," said Haggart, still eyeing the foolish farmer threateningly, "when I came back to Thrums. It just needed a touch to make it boil."

"And, sal, it got the touch!"

"Ay, I admit that; but no till the Monday."

We go back to the march from the Roods to Tillyloss. In less time than it would have taken Haggart to bring his sarcastic shaft from the depths where he stowed these things and fire it into Lookaboutyou, he had walked triumphantly to Tillyloss, and turned up the road that was presently to be named after him.

His tail of fellow-townsmen came to a stop at the pump, where they had a good view of Haggart's house, all but a few daring ones, nearly all women, who ran · up the dyke, in hope of witnessing the meeting with Chirsty.

"I suppose, lads," Haggart said to us, "that ye're thinking my arrival at Tillyloss was the crowning moment of my glory?"

"It was bound to be."

"So ye think, Andrew; but that just shows how little ye ken about the human heart. I got as far as Tillyloss terribly windy at the way ye had honored me; but, lads, something came ower me at sicht of that auld outside stair. Ay, it had a michty hame-like look."

"I've heard tell ye stopped and gazed at it, like grand folk admiring the view."

"Ay, lathies, I daursay I did so; but it wasna the view I was thinking about. I'll warrant ye couldna say what was in my mind?"

"Your funeral?"

"I never gave it a thocht. Na, but I'll tell ye: I was thinking of Chirsty Todd."

"Ay, and the startle she was to get?"

"No, Snecky; it's an astonishing thing, but the moment my e'en saw that outside stair I

completely lost heart, and frae being lifted up
with pride, down goes my courage like a bucket
in a well.   Was it the stair as terrified me ?
Na, it was Chirsty Todd.   Lads, I faced the
whole drove of ye as bold as a king sitting
down at the head of his tea table; but the
thocht of Chirsty Todd brocht my legs to a
stop.   Ay, for all we may say to the contrairy,
is there a man in Thrums as hasna a kind of
fear of his wife ? ”

At this question Haggart's listeners usually
looked different ways.

“ Lads,” continued Tammas, “ it ran through
me suddenly, like a cold blast of wind—‘ What
if Chirsty shouldna be glad to see me back ? ’
and I regretted michty that I hadna halved the
guineas with her.   Ay, I tell ye openly, as I
found mysel' getting smaller, like a gas-ball
with a hole in it, and I a kind of lost sight of
all I had to boast of.   I was ashamed of mysel'
and also in mortal terror of Chirsty Todd.
Ay, but I never let her ken that: na, na ; a
man has to be wary about what he tells his
wife.”

“ He has so, for she's sure to fling it at him
by and by like a wet clout.   Women has ter-

rible memories for what ye blurt out to them."

" Ye're repeating my words, Rob, as if they were your own; but what ye say is true. Women doesna understand about men's minds being profounder than theirs, and consequently waur to manage."

" That's so, and it's a truth ye daurna mention to them. But ye was come to the outside stair, Tammas."

" Ay, I was. Lads, I climbed that stair all of a tremble, and my hand was shaking so muckle that for a minute I couldna turn the handle of the door."

" We saw as ye a sort of tottered."

" Ay, I was uneasy ; and even when the door opened I didna just venture inside. Na, I had a feeling as it was a judicious thing to keep a grip of the door. Weel, lathies, I stood there keeking in, and what does I see but Chirsty Todd sitting into the fire, with my auld pipe in her mouth. Ay, there she sat blasting."

" How did that affect ye, Tammas? "

"How did it affect me? It angered me most michty to see her enjoying hersel', and me thocht to be no more."

" ' Ye heartless limmer,' I says to mysel', and that reminds me as a man is master in his own house, so I bangs the door to and walks in."

" Wha spoke first ? "

" Oh, I spoke first.　I spoke just as her een lichted on me."

" Ye had said a memorable thing ? "

" I canna say I did.　No, Pete.　I just gave her a sly kind of look, and I says, 'Ay, Chirsty.' "

" She screamed, they say ? "

" She did so, and the pipe fell from her mouth.　Ay, it's a gratification to me to ken that she did scream."

" And what happened next ? "

" She spyed at me suspiciously ; and says she, 'Tammas Haggart, are you in the flesh ?' to which I replies, 'I am so, Chirsty.' 'Then,' cries she sharply, 'take your dirty feet off my clean floor ! ' "

" And did ye ? "

" Ay, I put them on the fender ; and she cries, 'Take your dirty feet off the fender.'

" Lads, I thocht it was best to sing small, so I took off my boots, and she sat glowering at me, but never speaking.　'Ay, Chirsty,' I says, ' ye've had rain I'm thinking ; ' and

she says, ' The rain's neither here nor there ;
the question is, How did you break out?'
Ay, the crittur thocht I had broken out of my
grave."

" We all thocht that."

" Nat'rally ye did. Weel, I began my story
at the beginning, but with the impatience
of a woman she aye said, ' I dinna want to
hear that, I want to ken how you broke
out ! ' "

" But she wanted to hear about the siller in
the buttons ? "

" Ay, but I tried to slither ower the buttons, fearing she would be mad at me for
spending them. And, losh, mad she was ! I
explained to her as I put them to good use
by improving my mind, but she says, ' Dinna
blather about your mind to me, or I'll take
the poker to ye ! ' Chirsty was always fond
of language."

" But what about the Well-wisher ? "

" Oh, that was a queery. I says to Chirsty,
' I did not forget your sufferings, Chirsty, for
I'm the Well-wisher.' At first she didna understand, but then she minds and says, ' It
was you as sent that bit cheese with D.

Fittis, was it.?' Lads, then it came out as
the cheese was standing in the press un-
touched. Ay, I tore it in twa with my hands,
and out rolls the guinea. She had never
dreamed of there being siller in the cheese."

" Na, she was terrified to touch the cheese.
I mind when I could have bocht it frae her for
twa or three bawbees. Ay, what chances a
body misses. But she had been pleasanter
with ye after she got the guinea ? "

" I can hardly say that. She nipped it up
quick, and tells me to go on with my story.
Weel, I did so in a leisurely way, her aye nag-
ging at me to come to the quarry, as I soon had
to do. I need scarce tell ye she was michty
surprised it wasna me ye buried, but, after that
was cleared up, I saw her mind wasna on what
I was saying to her. No, lads, I was the
length of Dundee in my story when she jumps
up, and away she goes to the lowest shelf in
the dresser. I stopped in my talk and watched
her. She pulls out the iron and lays it on the
table, then she shoves a heater into the fire,
and brings an auld dicky out of a drawer.
Lads, I had a presentiment what she was
after."

" ' What are ye doing, Chirsty ? ' I says with misgivings.

" ' I'm to iron a dicky for ye to wear to-morrow,' she cries, and she kicks my foot off the fender.

" ' I'm no going to the kirk,' I warns her.

" ' Are ye no ? ' says she ; ' ye gang twice, Tammas Haggart, though the Auld Licht minister has to drive ye to the door with a stick.'

" Ay, when I heard she had joined the Auld Lichts I kent I was done with lazy Sabbaths. Weel, she ironed away at that dicky with tremendous energy, and then all at once she lays down the iron and she cries,

" ' Keeps us all, I had forgotten ! ' She was the picture of woe.

" What's the matter, Chirsty ? ' I says.

" ' She stood there wringing her hands.

" ' Ye canna gang to the kirk,' she moans, ' for ye have no clothes.'

" ' No clothes ! ' I cries. ' I have my blacks.'

" ' They're gone,' she says.

" ' Gone, ye limmer !' I says, ' wha has them ? '

6

" ' Davit Whamand,' she says ' has the coat,
and Hender Haggart the waistcoat and the
hat.'

" Ay, lads, I can tell ye this composedly
now, but I was fuming at the time. Chirsty's
passion for genteelity was such that she had
imitated grand folk's customs and given away
the clothes as had been worn by the corpse."

" That came of taking a wife frae Bal-·
ribbie."

" Ay, and it's not the only proof of Chirsty's
vanity, for, as ye all ken, she continued to
wear her crape to the kirk long after I came
back."

" Because she thocht it set her ? "

" Ou, rather, just because she had it. But
it was aggravating to me to have to walk with
her to the kirk, and her in widow's crapes. It
would have provoked an ordinary man to the
drink."

" It would so, but what said ye when ye
heard the blacks was gone ? "

" Said ? It wasna a time for saying. I
shoved my feet into my boots and flung on my
bonnet, and hurries to the door,

" ' Whaur are ye going ? ' cries Chirsty.

" ' To demand back my blacks,' I says, dashing open the door with my fist. Ye may mind there was some of ye keeking in at the door and the window, trying to hearken to the conversation."

" Ay, and we flew frae ye as if ye was the Riot Act. But we was thinking by that time as ye micht be a sort of living."

" Maybe, but I wasna thinking about you. Na, it was the blacks as was on my mind, and away I goes."

" Ye ran."

" Yes, I ran straight to the Tenements to Davit Whamand's house. Lads, I said the pot was very near the boil when I marched down the Roods, but my humor was getting cold again. Ay, Chirsty Todd had suddenly lifted the pot off the fire."

CHAPTER VI.

IN WHICH A BIRTH IS RECORDED.

" Davit's collie barked at me," Haggart continued, " when it heard me lifting the sneck of the door, but I cowed it with a stern look, and stepped inside. The wife was away cracking about me to Lizzie Linn, but there was Davit himsel with a bantam cock on his knee, the which was ailing, and he was forcing a little butter into its nib. He let the beast fall when he saw me, and I was angered to notice as he had been occupied with a bantam when he should have been discussing me with consternation."

" It was the greater surprise to him when in ye marched."

" Ay, but my desire to be thocht a ghost had gone, and I says ·at once, 'Dinna stand trembling there, Davit Whamand,' I says, ' for

I'm in the flesh, and so you'll please hand ower my black coat!' He hardly believed I was human at first, but at the mention of the coat he grows stiff and hard, and says he, 'What black coat?'

" ' Deception will not avail ye, Davit Whamand,' says I, ' for Chirsty has confessed all.'

" ' The coat's mine,' says Davit, glowering.

" ' I want that coat direct,' I says.

" ' Think shame o' yoursel',' says he, 'and you a corpse this half year.'

" The crittur tried to speak like a minister, but I waved away his argument with my hand.

" ' Back to the cemetery, ye shameless corp, says he, 'and I'll mention this to nobody; but if ye didna gang peaceably we'll call out the constables.'

" ' Dinna haver, Davit Whamand,' I retorts, ' for ye ken fine I'm in the flesh, and if ye dinna produce my coat immediately I'll take the law of ye.'

" ' Will ye?' he sneers; ' and what micht ye call yoursel?'

" ' I'll call mysel by my own name, namely, Tammas Haggart,' I thunders.

" ' Yea, yea,' says he; ' I'm thinking a corp hands on his name to his auldest son, and Tammas Haggart being dead without a son the name becomes extinct.'

" Lads, that did stagger me a minute, but then I minds I'm living, and I cries, ' Ye sly crittur, I'm no dead.'

" ' Are ye not ? ' says he; ' I think ye are.'

" ' Do I look dead ? ' I argues.

" ' Look counts for nothing before a bailie,' says he, ' and if ye annoy me I'll bring witnesses to prove you're dead. Yes, I'll produce the widow in her crapes, and them as coffined ye.'

" ' Ay,' I cries, ' but I'll produce mysel'.'

" ' The waur for you,' says he, ' for if ye try to overthrow the law we'll bury ye again, though it should be at the public expense.'

" Lads, that made me uneasy, and all I could think to do was just to fling out my foot at the bantam.

" ' Ye daur look me in the face, Davit Whamand,' I says, ' and pretend as I'm no mysel' ? '

" ' I daur do so,' he says; ' and not on'y are

ye no yersel', but I would never have recognized
ye for such.'

" ' So, so,' I remarks ; ' and ye refuse to
deliver up my coat ? '

" ' Yes,' he says, ' and what's more I never
had your coat.'

" Lads, that was his cautiousness in case twa
lines of defense was needed before the bailie ;
but I said no more to him, for now the house
began to fill with folk wanting to make sure of
me, and I was keen to convince them I was in
the flesh before Davit prejudiced them. Ay,
Robbie, you was one of them as convoyed me
to Hender Haggart's."

" I was, Tammas, and when ye shut the door
on me a mask of folk came round me to hear
how ye had broke out."

" I daursay that, but their curiosity didna
interest me now. Ye mind when we got to
Hender's house it was black and dark, him
pretending to be away to his bed ? Ay, but
the smell of roasting potatoes belied that. As
we ken now, Hender had been warned that I
was at Davit's demanding back the coat, and
he suspected I would come next to him for the
waistcoat and the hat."

" Ay, but he had to let ye in."

" Ou, I would have broken in the door rather than have been beat, and in the tail of the day Hender takes the snib off the door."

" He pretended he thocht ye a ghost too, did he no ? "

" No, no, that's a made up story. Hender and his wife had agreed to pretend that, but when Hender came to the door he became stupid-like, and when I says ' Ay, Hender,' he says ' Ay, Tammas.' I've heard his wife raged at him about it after.

" ' Nanny,' I says to the wife, ' it's me back again, and ye'll oblige by handing ower my waistcoat and my hat.'

" I've forgotten to tell ye that when I walked in, Nanny was standing on a stool with a poker in her hand, the which she was using to shove something on the top of the press out of sicht. She jumped down hurriedly, but looking bold, and says she, ' These mice is very troublesome.'

" Weel, I had a presentiment, and I says, ' Give me the poker, Nanny, and I'll get at the mice ! ' Says she, ' Na, na '; and she lifts away the stool.

" All this time Hender had been looking

very melancholy, but despite that, he was glad
to see me back, and he says in a sentimental
way, ' You're a stranger, Tammas,' says he.

"' I am, Hender,' says I, ' and I want my
waistcoat, also my hat.'

" Hender gave a confused look to the wife,
and says she, ' The waistcoat has been sold for
rags, and I gave the hat to tinklers.'

"' Hender Haggart,' says I, ' is this so ? '

" Hender a sort of winked, meaning that we
could talk the thing ower when Nanny wasna
there, but I couldna wait.

"' I think, Nanny,' says I, pointedly, ' as I'll
take a look at these mice of yours.'

"' Ye'll do no sich things,' says she.

"' I'm thinking,' says I, ' as I'll find a black
waistcoat on the top of that press, and likewise
a Sabbath hat.'

" Hender couldna help giving me an admiring look for my quickness, but Nanny put her
back to the press, and says she, ' Hender, am I
to be insulted before your face ? '

" Hender was perplexed, but he says to me,
' Ye hear what Nanny says, Tammas ? '

"' Ay,' I says, ' I hear her.'

"'He hears ye, Nanny,' says Hender.

" ' But I want my lawful possessions,' I cries.

" Hender hesitated again, but Nanny repeats, ' Hender, am I to be insulted before your face?'

" ' Dinna insult her before my face,' Hender whispers to me.

" 'I offer no insult,' I says, loud out, ' but I've come for my waistcoat and my hat, and I dinna budge till I get them.'

" ' Ye've a weary time before ye, then,' says Nanny.

" ' I wonder ye wouldna be ashamed to keep a man frae his belongings,' I said.

" ' Tell him they're yours, Hender,' she cries.

" ' Ye see, Tammas,' says Hender, ' she says they're mine.'

" ' Ay,' I says, ' but ye canna pretend they're yours yersel', Hender ? '

" ' Most certainly ye can, Hender,' says Nanny.

" ' Ye see that, Tammas,' says Hender, triumphant.

" ' And how do ye make out as they are yours ? ' I asks him.

" ' Tell him,' cries Nanny, ' as ye got them for helping in his burial.'

" ' Tammas,' says Hender, ' that's how I got them.'

" ' Maybe,' I says, ' but did I give ye them ?

" ' Say he was a corp,' Nanny cries.

" ' Meaning no disrespect, Tammas,' says Hender, ' ye was a corp.'

" ' How could I have been a corp,' I argues, ' when here I am speaking to ye ? '

" Hender turned to Nanny for the answer to this, but she showed him her back, so he just said in a weak way, ' We'll leave the minister to settle that.'

" ' Hender, ye gowk,' I says, ' ye ken I'm living ; and if I'm living I'm no dead.'

" Lads, I regretted I hadna put it plain like that to Davit Whamand. However, Hender hadna the clear-headedness necessary to follow out sich reasoning, and he replies,

" ' No doubt,' he says, ' ye are living in a sense, but no in another sense.'

" ' I wasna the corp,' I cried.

" ' Weel, weel, Tammas,' says he, in a fell dignified voice, ' we needna quarrel on a matter of opinion.'

" I was just beginning to say as it was more likely to be the waistcoat we would fall out about, when in walks Chirsty in the most flurried way.

" ' Tammas Haggart,' she pants, ' come hame this instant ; the minister's waiting for ye.'

" Which minister ? " I asks.

" ' None other,' she says, looking proudly at Nancy, ' than the Auld Licht minister.'

" Lads, I shook in my boots at that, and I says, ' I winna come till I've got my hat and my waistcoat.'

" ' What,' screams Chirsty, ' ye daur to keep the minister waiting ! ' and she shoved me clean out of the house."

What the minister said to Haggart is not known, for Tammas never divulged the conversation. Those who remained on the watch said that the minister looked very stern when walking back to the manse, and that Chirsty found her husband tractable for the rest of the evening. The most we ever got out of Tammas on the subject was that though he had met many terrifying folk in his wanderings, they were a herd of sheep compared to the minister. He had sometimes to be enticed out

of the reverie into which thought of the minister plunged him.

"So it was next day ye dandered up to the
grave?" we would say craftily, though well
aware that he did not leave the house till
Monday.

"Na, na, not on the Sabbath day. When I
wakened in the morning I admit I was terribly
anxious to see the grave, as was natural, but
thocht of the minister cowed me. I would
have ventured as far as the grave if I had been
able to persuade mysel' I wasna going for
pleasure, but pleasure it was, lads. Ay, there
was no denying that."

"Chirsty was at the kirk?"

"She was so, and in her widow's crapes. I
watched her frae the window. Ay, it's no
everybody as has watched his own widow."

"Na, and it had been an impressive spectacle.
How would ye say she looked, Tammas?"

"She looked proud, Robbie."

"She would; but what would ye say she
was proud of?"

"Ah, Robbie, there you beat me. But I can
tell ye what she was proud of on the Monday."

"What?"

" Before porridge-time no less than seven
women, namely, three frae Tillyloss, twa frae
the Tenements, and twa frae the Roods, chaps
at the door and invites her to a dish of tea.
That's what she was proud of, and I would like
to hear of ony other woman in this town, single
or married or a widow, as has had seven invitations to her tea in one day."

" The thing's unparalleled ; but of course it
was to hear about you that they speired her ? "

" Oh, of course, and also to get out of her
what the minister said to me. Ay, but can
ony of ye tell me what's the memorablist thing
about these invitations ?"

"I dinna say I can, but it's something about
the grave."

" It's this, Snecky, that before Chirsty had
made up her mind whether to risk seven teas
in one day, I had become a humorist for life."

"Man, man, oh, losh ! "

" Ay, and it's perfectly appalling to consider
as she was so excited about her invitations that
when I came down frae the cemetery she never
looked me in the face, and I had to say to her,
' Chirsty Todd, do ye no see as something has
come ower me ?'   At that she says, ' I notice

you're making queer faces, but I dinna ken
what they mean.' ˉ 'They mean, Chirsty Todd,'
says I, 'as I am now a humorist,' to which she
replies, 'Pick up that dish-clout.' "

"Keep us all! But oh, man, a woman's
mind doesna easily rise to the sublime."

"It doesna, Pete, and I'll tell ye the reason;
it's because of women, that is to say, richt-
minded women, all having sich an adoration
for ministers."

"I dinna contradict ye, Tammas, but surely
that's a fearsome statement. Is ministers not
nearer the sublime than other folk?"

"They are, they are, and that's just it.
Ministers, ye may say, is always half road up
to the sublime. Weel, what's the result?
Women raises their een to gaze upon the sublime, when they catch sicht of the minister,
and canna look ony higher."

"Sal, Tammas, you've solved it! But I
warrant ye couldna have said that till ye became
a humorist?"

"No more than you could have said it yersel',
Robbie."

"Na, I dinna pretend I could have said it,
and even though I was to gang hame now and

say it in your very words, it wouldna have the same show as when you say it."

"It would not, for ye would just blurt it out, but them as watches me saying a humorous thing notices the mental struggle before the words comes up. Ay, the mental struggle's like the servant in grand houses as puts his head in at the door and cries, 'Leddies and gentlemen, take your seats, for the dinner is all but ready.'"

Early on Monday morning Haggart, the non-humorist, woke for the last time. The day was moderately fine, but gave no indication that anything remarkable was about to happen. Lookaboutyou, it is true, says that he noticed a queer stillness in the air, and Snecky Hobart spoke of an unusually restless night. It is believed by some that the cocks of Tillyloss did not crow that morning. But none of these phenomena were noticed until it became natural to search the memory for them, and Haggart himself always said that it was a common day. The fact, I suppose, is that an uncommon day was not needed, for here was Haggart and there was the cemetery. Nature never wastes her materials.

Haggart was elated no doubt, but so would any man have been in the circumstances. For the last time Haggart, the non-humorist, put off cleaning his boots for another day. For the last time he combed his hair without studying the effect in the piece of glass that was glued to the wall. Never again would the Haggart who briskly descended his outside stair, forgetting to shut the door, enter that room in which Chirsty was already baking bannocks. It was a new Haggart who would return presently, Haggart of Haggart's Roady, Haggart of Thrums, in short, Haggart the humorist.

The last person to speak to Haggart, the non-humorist, was James Spens, the last to see him was Sanders Landels. Jamie met him at the foot of Tillyloss, and Sanders passed him on the burying-ground brae. Both were ordinary persons, and they never distinguished themselves again.

It was not his grave that made Haggart a humorist, but the gravestone. Two years earlier he had erected a tombstone to the memory of his relatives, but it had never struck him that he would some day be able to read his

7

own fate on it.   The grave is to the right of
the entrance to the cemetery, almost exactly
under the favorite seat known as the Bower,
and being at the bend of the path it comes suddenly into view.   Haggart walked eagerly along
the path, an ordinary man upon the whole;
then all at once . . . . . .   He looked . . . . . .
He looked again.   This is what he read:

THIS STONE WAS ERECTED BY
THOMAS HAGGART
TO THE MEMORY OF PETER HAGGART,
FATHER OF THE SAID THOMAS,
WHO DEPARTED THIS LIFE, JAN. 7, 1825.
ALSO HERE LIES JEAN LINN, OR HAGGART,
MOTHER OF THE SAID THOMAS,
DIED 1828.
ALSO JEAN HAGGART,
SISTER OF THE SAID THOMAS,
DIED 1829.
ALSO ANDREW HAGGART,
BROTHER OF THE SAID THOMAS,
DIED 1831.
ALSO THE SAID THOMAS HIMSELF,
DIED 1834.

Haggart sat down on the grave.   In Thrums
common folk were doing common things—weav-

ing, feeding the hens, supping porridge, carting peats.

Haggart sat on the grave. In Thrums they were thinking of their webs, of their dinner, of well-scrubbed floors, of their love affairs.

But Haggart sat on the grave, and a pot began to boil. He has told us what happened. Down in his inside something was roaring, and every moment the noise increased. He breathed with difficulty. He was as a barrel swelling but held in by hoops of iron. He rose to his feet, for his tongue was hot and there was a hissing in his throat, and the iron hoops pressed more and more tightly. Suddenly the hissing ceased, and he stood as still as salt. The roaring far down died away. All at once he was tilted to the side, the hoops burst, and he began to laugh. The pot was boiling. Haggart was a humorist.

As soon as he realized what had happened Haggart returned to Tillyloss. The first to see him was Tibbie Robbie, the first to speak to him was William Lamb, the first to notice the change was Snecky Hobart.

I only undertook to tell how Haggart became

a humorist, and here therefore my story ends. I have shown how a lamp was lit in Thrums, but not how it burned.   Perhaps if I followed Haggart to his end, as I should like to do, to the time when the lamp flickered and a room in the Tenements grew dark, some who have smiled at an old man's tale would leave a tear behind them to a weaver's memory.

" Na," Haggart often said, " we winna touch the gravestone.   It'll come in handy some day."

His humor, appetizing from the first, ripened with the years.   For a time this was his comment on the tombstone :—

" Lads, lads, what a do we're preparing for posterity."

Later in his life he said,

" It's almost cruel to cheat future generations in this way."

His hair was white before he said,

" I dinna ken but what I should do the honest thing, and have the date rubbed out."

And when there was a squeal in his voice, he could add,

" No that it much matters."

HOW GAVIN BIRSE PUT IT TO MAG LOWNIE.

In a wet day the rain gathers in blobs on the road that passes our Thrums garden. Then it crawls into the cart-tracks, until the road is streaked with water. Last, the water gathers in heavy yellow pools. If the rain still continues, clods of earth topple from the garden dyke into the ditch.

On such a day, when even the dulseman had gone into shelter, and the women scudded by with their wrappers over their heads, came Gavin Birse to our door. Gavin, who is the Glen Quharity post, is still young, but has never been quite the same man since some amateurs in the Glen ironed his back for rheumatism. At present I am lodging in Thrums, with Hendry M'Qumpha, and I thought Gavin had called to have a crack with me. He sent his compliments up to the attic, however, by Leeby, and would I come and be a witness?

Gavin came up and explained. He had taken off his scarf and thrust it into his pocket, lest the rain should take the color out of it. His boots cheeped, and his shoulders had risen to his ears. He stood steaming before my fire.

"If it's no ower muckle to ask ye," he said, "I would like ye for a witness."

"A witness! But for what do you need a witness, Gavin?"

"I want ye," he said, "to come wi' me to Mag's, and be a witness."

Gavin and Mag Birse had been engaged for a year or more. Mag is the daughter of Janet Ogilvy, who is best remembered as the body that took the hill (that is, wandered about it) for twelve hours on the day Mr. Dishart, the Auld Licht minister, accepted a call to another church.

"You don't mean to tell me, Gavin," I asked, "that your marriage is to take place to-day?"

By the twist of his mouth I saw that he was only deferring a smile.

"Far frae that," he said.

" Ah, then, you have quarreled, and I am to speak up for you ? "

" Na, na," he said, " I dinna want ye to do that above all things. It would be a favor if ye could gi'e me a bad character."

This beat me, and, I daresay, my face showed it.

" I'm no' juist what ye would call anxious to marry Mag noo," said Gavin, without a tremor.

I told him to go on.

" There's a lassie oot at Craigiebuckle," he explained, " workin' on the farm—Jeanie Luke by name. Ye may ha'e seen her ? "

" What of her ? " I asked, severely.

" Weel," said Gavin, still unabashed, " I'm thinkin' noo 'at I would rather ha'e her."

Then he stated his case more fully.

" Ay, I thocht I liked Mag oncommon till I saw Jeanie, an' I like her fine yet, but I prefer the other ane. That state o' matters canna gang on forever, so I came into Thrums the day to settle 't one wy or another."

" And how," I asked, " do you propose going about it ? It is a somewhat delicate business."

"Ou, I see nae great difficulty in't. I'll speir at Mag, blunt oot, if she'll let me aff. Yes, I'll put it to her plain."

" You're sure Jeanie would take you ? "

" Ay ; oh, there's nae fear o' that."

" But if Mag keeps you to your bargain ? "

" Weel, in that case there's nae harm done."

" You are in a great hurry, Gavin ? "

" Ye may say that ; but I want to be married. The wifie I lodge wi' canna last lang, an' I would like to settle doon in some place."

" So you are on your way to Mag's now ? "

" Ay, we'll get her in atween twal' and ane."

" Oh, yes ; but why do you want me to go with you ? "

" I want ye for a witness. If she winna let me aff, weel and guid ; and if she will, it's better to ha'e a witness in case she should go back on her word."

Gavin made his proposal briskly, and as coolly as if he were only asking me to go fishing ; but I did not accompany him to Mag's. He left the house to look for another witness, and about an hour afterwards Jess saw him pass with Tammas Haggart. Tammas cried in during the evening to tell us how the mission prospered.

"Mind ye," said Tammas, a drop of water hanging to the point of his nose, "I disclaim all responsibility in the business. I ken Mag weel for a thrifty, respectable woman, as her mither was afore her, and so I said to Gavin when he came to speir me."

"Ay, mony a pirn has Lisbeth filled to me," said Hendry, settling down to a reminiscence.

"No to be ower hard on Gavin," continued Tammas, forestalling Hendry, "he took what I said in guid part; but aye when I stopped speaking to draw breath, he says, 'The question is, will ye come wi' me?' He was michty made up in 's mind."

"Weel, ye went wi' him," suggested Jess, who wanted to bring Tammas to the point.

"Ay," said the stone-breaker, "but no in sic a hurry as that."

He worked his mouth round and round, to clear the course, as it were, for a sarcasm.

"Fowk often say," he continued, "'at 'am quick beyond the ordinar' in seein' the humorous side o' things."

Here Tammas paused, and looked at us.

" So ye are, Tammas," said Hendry. " Losh, ye mind hoo ye saw the humorous side o' me wearin' a pair o' boots 'at wisna marrows ! No, the ane had a toe-piece on, an' the other hadna."

" Ye juist wore them sometimes when ye was delvin'," broke in Jess, " ye have as guid a pair o' boots as ony in Thrums."

" Ay, but I had worn them," said Hendry, " at odd times for mair than a year, an' I had never seen the humorous side o' them. Weel, as fac as death (here he addressed me), Tammas had just seen them twa or three times when he saw the humorous side o' them. Syne I saw their humorous side, too, but no till Tammas pointed it oot."

"That was naething," said Tammas, "naething ava to some things I've done."

" But what aboot Mag ? " said Leeby.

" We wasna that length, was we ? "said Tammas. " Na, we was speakin' aboot the humorous side. Ay, wait a wee, I didna mention the humorous side for naething."

He paused to reflect.

" Oh, yes," he said at last, brightening up, "I was sayin' to ye hoo quick I was to see the humorous side o' onything. Ay, then, what

made me say that was 'at in a clink (flash) I saw
the humorous side o' Gavin's position."

" Man, man," said Hendry, admiringly, " and
what is 't ? "

" Oh, it's this, there's something humorous in
speirin' a woman to let ye aff so as ye can be
married to another woman."

"I daursay there is," said Hendry, doubtfully.

" Did she let him aff ? " asked Jess, taking
the words out of Leeby's mouth.

" I'm comin' to that,' said Tammas.   " Gavin
proposes to me after I had had my laugh———"

" Yes," cried Hendry, banging the table with
his fist, " it has a humorous side.   Ye're richt
again, Tammas."

" I wish ye wadna blatter (beat) the table,"
said Jess, and then Tammas proceeded.

" Gavin wanted me to tak' paper an' ink an'
a pen wi' me, to write the proceedin's doon, but
I said, ' Na, na, I'll tak' paper, but no nae ink
nor nae pen, for there'll be ink an' a pen there.'
That was what I said."

" An' did she let him aff ? " asked Leeby.

" Weel," said Tammas, " aff we goes to Mag's
hoose, an' sure enough Mag was in.   She was
alane, too ; so Gavin, no to waste time, juist sat

doon for politeness' sake, an' syne rises up again;
an' says he, 'Marget Lownie, I ha'e a solemn
question to the speir at ye, namely this, Will
you, Marget Lownie, let me, Gavin Birse, aff?'"

" Mag would start at that ? "

" Sal, she was braw an' cool. I thocht she
mun ha'e got wind o' his intentions aforehand,
for she just replies, quiet-like, ' Hoo do ye
want aff, Gavin ? ' "

" ' Because,' says he, like a book, ' my
affections has undergone a change.'

" ' Ye mean Jean Luke,' says Mag.

" ' That is wha I mean,' says Gavin, very
straitforrard."

" But she didna let him aff, did she ? "

" Na, she wasna the kind. Says she, ' I
wonder to hear ye, Gavin, but 'am no goin'
to agree to naething o' that sort.'

" ' Think it ower,' says Gavin.

" ' Na, my mind's made up,' said she.

" ' Ye would sune get anither man,' he
says, earnestly.

" ' Hoo do I ken that?' she speirs, rale
seriously, I thocht, for men's no sae easy to
get.

" ' Am sure o't,' Gavin says, wi' michty

conviction in his voice, 'for ye're bonny to
look at, an' weel-kent for bein' a guid body.'

"'Ay,' says Mag, 'I'm glad ye like me,
Gavin, for ye have to tak me.'"

"That put a clincher on him," interrupted
Hendry.

" He was loth to gie in," replied Tammas,
so he says, ' Ye think 'am a fine character,
Marget Lownie, but ye're very far mista'en.
I wouldna wonder but what I was lossin' my
place some o' thae days, an' syne whaur would
ye be ?—Marget Lownie,' he goes on, ' 'am
nat'rally lazy and fond o' the drink. As sure
as ye stand there, 'am a reglar deevil! '

" That was strong language," said Hendry,
" but he would be wantin to fleg (frighten) her?"

" Just so, but he didna manage 't, for Mag
says, ' We a' ha'e oor faults, Gavin, an' deevil
or no de'vil, ye 're the man for me! '

" Gavin thocht a bit," continued Tammas,
"an' syne he tries her on a new tack. ' Marget
Lownie,' he says, ' ye're father's an auld man
noo, an' he has naebody but yersel' to look
after him. I'm thinkin' it would be kind o'
cruel o' me to tak ye awa frae him?'"

" Mag wouldna be ta'en in wi' that; she

wasna born on a Sawbath," said Jess, using one
of her favorite sayings.

"She wasna," answered Tammas. "Says
she, 'Hae nae fear on that score, Gavin ; my
father's fine willin' to spare me !'"

"An' that ended it ?"

"Ay, that ended it."

"Did ye tak it doon in writin' ?" asked
Hendry.

"There was nae need," said Tammas, handing round his snuff-mull. "No, I never
touched paper. When I saw the thing was
settled I left them to their coortin'. They're
to tak a look at Snecky Hobart's auld hoose
the nicht. It's to let."

LIFE IN A COUNTRY MANSE.

CHAPTER I.

JANET.

Up here among the heather (or nearly so)
we are, in the opinion of tourists, a mere hamlet, though to ourselves we are at least a
village. Englishmen call us a " clachan "—
though, truth to tell, we are not sure what
that is. Just as Gulliver could not see the
Lilliputians without stooping, these tourists
may be looking for the clachan when they
are in the middle of it, and knocking at one
of its doors to ask how far they have yet to go
till they reach it. To be honest, we are only
five houses in a row (including the smiddy),
with a Free Church manse and a few farms
here and there on the hillsides.

So far as the rest of the world is concerned,
we are blotted out with the first fall of snow.
I suppose tourists scarcely give us a thought
save when they are here. I have heard them
admiring our glen in August, and adding :

"But what a place it must be in winter !"

To this their friends reply, shivering :

" A hard life, indeed ! "

And the conversation ends with the comment :

" Don't call it life ; it is merely existence."

Well, it would be dull, no doubt, for tourists
up here in January, say, but I find the winter
a pleasant change from summer. I am the
minister, and though my heart sank when I
was " called," I rather enjoy the life now. I
am the man whom the tourists pity most.

" The others drawl through their lives,"
these tourists say, " to the manner born ; but
think of an educated man who has seen life
spending his winters in such a place ! "

" He can have no society."

"Let us hope the poor fellow is married."

" Oh, he is sure to be. But, married or
single, I am certain I would go mad if I were
in his shoes."

Their comparison is thrown away. I am strong and hale. I enjoy the biting air, and I seldom carry an umbrella. I should perhaps go mad if I were in the Englishmen's shoes, glued to a stool all day, and feeling my road home through fog at night. And there is many an educated man who envies me. Did not three times as many probationers apply for a hearing when the church was vacant as could possibly be heard?

But how do I occupy my time? the English gentlemen would say, if they had not forgotten me. What do the people do in winter? True, I don't lie long in the mornings and doze on the sofa in the afternoon, and go to bed at one o'clock. When I was at College, where I saw much " life," I breakfasted frequently at ten; but here, where time must (they say) hang heavy on my hands, I am up at seven. Though I am not a married man, no one has said openly that I am insane. Janet, my housekeeper and servant, has my breakfast of porridge and tea and ham ready by half-past seven sharp. You see the mornings are keen, and so, as I have no bedroom fire nor hot water, I dress much more quickly

8

than I dressed at College. Six minutes I give myself, than Janet and I have prayers, and then follows my breakfast. What an appetite I have! I am amazed to recall the student days, when I " could not look at porridge," and thought a halfpenny roll sufficient for two of us.

Dreary pleasure, you say, breakfasting alone in a half-furnished house, with the snow lying some feet deep outside and still monotonously falling. Do I forget the sound of my own voice between Monday and Saturday? I should think not. Nor do I forget Janet's voice. I have read somewhere that the Scotch are a very taciturn race, but Janet is far more Scotch than the haggis that is passed round at some London dinners, and Janet is not a silent woman. The difficulty with some servants is to get them to answer your summons, but my difficulty with Janet is to get her back to the kitchen. Her favorite position is at the door, which she keeps half open. One of her feet she twists round it, and there she stands, half out of the room and half in it. She has a good deal of gossip to tell me about those five houses that lie low, two hundred yards from the manse, and it must be admitted that I listen. Why not? If one is interested in people he must gossip about them. You, in London, may not care in the least who your next door neighbor is, but you gossip about your brothers and sisters and aunts. Well, my people are as familiar to me as your brothers are to you, and, therefore, I say, " Ah, indeed," when told that the smith is busy with the wheel of a certain farmer's cart, and " Dear me, is that so ? " when Janet explains that William, the ploughman, has got Meggy, his wife, to cut his hair. Meggy has cut my own hair. She puts a bowl on my head and clips away everything that it does not cover. So I would miss Janet if she were gone, and her tongue is as enlivening as a strong ticking clock. No doubt there are times when, if I were not a minister, I might fling something soft at her. She shows to least advantage when I have visitors, and even in winter I have a man to dinner now and again. Then I realize that Janet does not know her place. While we are dining she hovers in the vicinity. If she is not pretending to put the room to rights, she is in her fortified position at the door ; and if she is not at the door she is immediately behind it.

Her passion is to help in the conversation. As she brings in the potatoes she answers the last remark my guest addressed to me, and if I am too quick for her she explains away my answer, or modifies it, or signifies her approval of it.   Then I try to be dignified, and to show Janet her place. If I catch her eye I frown, but such opportunities are rare, for it is the guest on whom she concentrates herself. She even tells him, in my presence, little things about myself which I would prefer to keep to myself. The impression conveyed by her is that I confide everything to her. When my guest remarks that I am becoming a hardened bachelor, and I hint that it is because the ladies do not give me a chance, Janet breaks in with——

"Oh, 'deed it's a wonder he wasn't married long since, but the one he wanted wouldn't have him, and the ones that want him he won't take. He's an ill man to please."

"Ah, Janet," the guest may say (for he enjoys her interference more than I do), "you make him so comfortable that you spoil him."

"Maybe," says Janet, "but it took me years to learn how to manage him."

" Does he need to be managed ? "

" I never knew a man that didna."

Then they get Janet to tell them all my little " tantrums " (as she calls them), and she holds forth on my habit of mislaying my hat and then blaming her, or on how I hate rice pudding, or on the way I have worn the carpet by walking up and down the floor when I would be more comfortable in a chair. Now and again I have wound myself up to the point of reproving Janet when the guest had gone, but the result is that she tells her select friends how " quick in the temper "· I am. So Janet must remain as she has grown, and it is gratifying to me (though I don't let on) to know that she turns up her nose at every other minister who preaches in my church. Janet is always afraid when I go off for a holiday that the congregations in the big towns will " snap me up." It is pleasant to feel that she has this opinion of me, though I know that the large congregations do not share it.

Who are my winter visitors ? The chief of them is the doctor. We have no doctor, of course, up here, and this one has to come twelve miles to us. He is rather melancholy when we send for him ; but he wastes no time in coming, though he may not have had his clothes off for twenty-four hours, and is well aware that we cannot pay big fees. Several times he has had to remain with me all night, and once he was snowed up here for a week. At times, too, he drives so far on his way to us and then has to turn back because the gig sticks on the heavy roads. He is only a doctor in a small country town, but I am elated when I see him, for he can tell me whether the Government is still in power. Then I have the school inspector once a year. The school inspector is always threatening to change the date of inspection to summer, but he takes the town from which the doctor comes in early spring, and finds it convenient to come from there to here. Early spring is often winter with us, so that the school inspector comes when there is usually snow on the ground or threatening. The school is a mile away at another " clachan," but the inspector dines with me, and so does the schoolmaster. On these occasions the schoolmaster is not such good company as at other times, for he is anxious about his passes, and explains (as I think) more than is necessary that regular attendance is out of the question in a place like this. The inspector's visit is the time of my great annual political debate, for the doctor calls politics " fudge." The inspector and I are on different sides, however, and we go at each other hammer and tongs, while the schoolmaster signs to me (with his foot) not to anger the inspector.

Of course, outsiders will look incredulous when I assure them that a good deal of time is passed in preparing my sermons. I have only one Sabbath service, but two sermons, the one beginning as soon as the other is finished. In such a little church, you will say, they must be easily pleased; but they are not. Some of them tramp long distances to church in weather that would keep you, reader, in the house, though your church is round the corner and there is pavement all the way to it. I can preach old sermons? Indeed I cannot. Many of my hearers adjourn to one of the five houses when the service is over, and there I am picked pretty clean. They would detect an old sermon at once, and resent it. I do not " talk " to them from the pulpit. I write my sermons in the manse, and though I use " paper," the less I use it the better they are pleased.

The visits of the doctor are pleasant to me in one sense, but painful in others, for I need not say that when he is called I am required too. To wade through miles of snow is no great hardship to those who are accustomed to it; but the heavy heart comes when one of my people is seriously ill. Up here we have few slight illnesses. The doctor cannot be summoned to attend them, and we usually "fight away" until the malady has a heavy hold. Then the doctor comes, and though we are so scattered, his judgment is soon known all through the glens. When the tourists come back in summer they will not see all the "natives" of the year before.

It is said by those who know nothing of our lives that we have no social events worth speaking of, and no amusements. This is what ignorance brings ousiders to. I had a marriage last week that was probably more exciting than many of your grand affairs in London. And as for amusements, you should see us gathered together in the smiddy, and sometimes in the schooi-house. But I must break off here, for the reason that I have used up all my spare sermon paper—a serious matter. I shall send the editor something about our social gatherings presently, for he says he wants it. Janet, I may add, has discovered that this is not a sermon, and is very curious about it.

CHAPTER II.

JANET'S CURIOSITY.

I HAD no intention of saying anything more about our "clachan," but since I posted my two last letters Janet has been so miserable, entirely owing to her reprehensible inquisitiveness, that I have been quite uncomfortable in the manse. If this is printed, as a kind of postscript to what I wrote before, I shall read it aloud to Janet, and so, I hope, humiliate her.

I hinted that Janet could not discover why I was writing so much. At first she thought I was at sermons, but very soon she decided against this theory. Without blushing—the woman cannot blush—she would look over my shoulder and gaze at the paper ; but that helped her not a jot, for Janet cannot read what she calls "wrote hand."

"Ay, Janet," I would say to her when I looked behind me and found her eyes on the paper, "and how do you like it ?"

" 'Deed," she would reply, " I dinna like it at all, and I think you would be better employed attending to your duties."

" How do you know I am not at this moment attending to my duties ? "

" Very well ; I canna read your wrote hand, but I see it's not a sermon you're at."

I was curious to know how Janet had discovered this, and pressed her.

" You scrawl your sermons, for one thing," said Janet, " and that is wrote plainer."

" And for another ? "

" Well, for another I've seen you smiling to yourself when you were writing, and there's nothing to smile at in your sermons."

" Any more reasons ? "

" Yes, there's this. When I came in yesterday and told you your supper was ready you wrote on for half an hour, so that I had to put your porridge in the oven to warm. You're very willing to come to your supper when it's just a sermon you're at."

This, of course, is utterly untrue, and I told Janet to leave the room, which she did, banging the door.

Janet thought it out doubtless in the kitchen,

and her next idea was that I was to be called
to Aberdeen.   I had been in Aberdeen just before the winter came on, and she decided that
I was writing out my testimonials.   It is not,
however, Janet's way to question me boldly on
any matter that she thinks I want to keep
secret.   If she had asked me whether I was expecting to be called away I would have told
her the truth, but what she did was this.   She
"stepped down " to the smiddy, and informed
the smith's wife that I had received a call from
Aberdeen.   Janet thinks she has an official
connection with the Free Church because she
is my housekeeper, and she likes to be first in
the field with church news.   It is wormwood
to her to discover that the elders have been
told anything by me which I have not first told
her, and so she is constantly forming absurd
conclusions, and announcing them as facts.
Of course, the smith's wife told her neighbors
that I had a call to Aberdeen, and soon the
glen was discussing nothing else.   The session
came to the manse to hear all about it, and I
had to tell them that the story was only another
of Janet's foolish notions.   I was very angry
with Janet, but she was not in the least ashamed

of herself. If I had not got a call, who was I writing these letters to? she asked herself. Her next decision was that I was to be married. This enraged her. The fact that I posted the letters myself struck her as proof positive. Of course, I only posted them because I knew that if I gave them to her she would get some one to read the address.

This time Janet kept her suspicions to herself, leading me, however, to understand that I was behaving very foolishly.

" You'll have been hearing," she would say, " that the schoolmaster and his wife are getting on very ill ? "

" On the contrary, I understand that they are very happy."

"Some folk have queer ideas of happiness, but I would not be happy if I was a schoolmaster, and my wife flung the tongs at me."

" Tuts, tuts, Janet, that never happened at the school-house."

" Did it not ? " said Janet. " You can see the mark of the tongs on his brow."

Then Janet would look sideways at me, and say artfully :

" She's an Aberdeen woman."

" So I believe."

" Ay, the Aberdeen lassies is sly."

" What makes you think that ? "

" It's well known. I've often heard them that kens say that you can just be sure of one thing about Aberdeen lassies."

" And what is that ? "

" That they're the very opposite of what they pretend to be."

With this shot Janet would retire, but soon she would return to the subject.

" I hear thae Aberdeen lassies try terrible hard to snap up the students."

" Do they ? "

" They do, and they have ruined many a promising man—especially ministers."

" But many a minister is married without being ruined."

" Not to an Aberdeen lassie.   These limmers are no' brought up to mak' housekeepers, but just to show off.   They can play on the piano, and that's about all they're fit for.   They would disgrace a manse, leastwise a country manse."

" They would have had no chance with you, Janet, if you had been a man."

" They wouldna; but some folk are no' difficult to get round, and ministers are easily wheedled."

"You don't think me easily wheedled, do you? "

" 'Deed there's no saying."

" But if I had been so week I would have fallen a victim to their wiles long ago."

" I dinna ken about that. It's said there's no fule like an old fule."

" Do you mean to call me old ? "

" Oh, you're no' that young now."

" What makes you talk so much about marriage nowadays, Janet?"

" I have een, and can use them. When I see you writing letters by the hour I ken what it means."

" But if I'm writing to a lady, why does she not write to me ? "

" That's what puzzles me, but no doubt she's sly. She kens what she's about. I daresay she has another lad she would rather have, and she's just keeping you dangling on, in case he refuses her."

" Refuses her, Janet? The woman, as you surely know, does not propose to the man."

" I'm thinking she does a hantle times oftener than the men have any idea of. Ye may
laugh, but I ken women—especially these
Aberdeen hussies."

" Why, you never were within seventy miles
of Aberdeen in your life."

" Maybe no, but I ken what fules these
women mak' of ministers. Yes, and I ken
how the ministers repents when it's too late.
You admire these dressed-up dolls' grand
clothes, but I'm thinking you sing a different
tune when you have to pay for them. The
piano's a pretty instrument, but you think less
of it when you're hungry and the broth pot's
full of soot."

" But, Janet, the Aberdeen lassie would
keep a servant to look after the broth pot."

" And a pretty-like servant, I'm thinking.
These limmers of stuck-up wives dinna like to
have a respectable middle-aged woman in the
kitchen like——"

" Like yourself ? "

" Yes, like myself. Oh, no; they bring
some useless fule of a lassie with them that
they think genteel-looking. Yes, she can
wear a neat cap (and set it at every single man

in the kirk); but as for work, she kens nothing about it. All she's fit for is for combing
her mistress's false hair and burning the
potatoes."

"Hoots, Janet, you were young once yourself."

"Oh, you're an infatuated man, and will
not listen to reason. But let me tell you this,
that folk haver when they say a minister is
better looked after when he's married. That's
a story invented by young women. When
you have ministers preaching here, do you
think I need to speir whether they're married
or single? No, I ken from one look at them.
If they're sensible single men with a decent
body to look after them, their boots is in good
order and their coats well brushed. But I
detect the married man at once by his want of
buttons and his boots worn down at the heel,
and the seams of his sleeves open. Yes, and
I ken him by his want of spirit. However, as
I say, willful man maun have his say, and I
will not argue with you."

Then one day Janet found out that my letters
had been addressed to a newspaper office, and
immediately she had a new idea. I was adver-

tising for another housekeeper. This was too terrible, and she could beat about the bush no longer. She walked into the manse parlor, and said:

"I dinna ken what I've done to make you treat me so secret-like, but I want to hear the worst."

"What are you talking about, Janet?" I asked, innocently.

"Are you to be married?" demanded Janet.

"Certainly not," I answered. "No one will have me."

"Then it's a new servant?"

"What is a new servant?"

"That you're advertising for."

"Did I say I was advertising?"

"Tell me the worst, I can hear it."

"Janet," I said, severely, "your curiosity will bring you to an early grave if you don't restrain it. It is no affair of yours what I have been writing, and therefore I shall not answer your questions. You have brought all your misery on yourself."

So Janet is still wondering what the writing is about, but I won't tell her till the paper arrives. Then I shall read this aloud to her, and add certain moral reflections which will cow her for a day or two, though they would not interest the public.

CHAPTER III.

TEACHER M'QUEEN.

As I tried to show some time ago, my old manse housekeeper, Janet, takes a personal interest in my affairs. In certain matters she has me under complete subjection; for instance, I dare not smoke (except in company) in my black coat, and it is the worse for me if I forget to change my socks on the days which she has, as it were, set apart for that purpose. So far she has allowed me to compose my own sermons, but I have visions of a time when she will insist on telling me what to say in the pulpit, as well as how to say it. Nay, more, Teacher M'Queen declared at the smiddy the other night that when I grew old and weak in intellect (Janet, who dislikes him, says that he said " weaker in intellect ") my housekeeper would propose to me, and we would be " kirked " before I had courage to enter a protest. This prediction I openly flout, while admitting Janet's power in the manse. This chapter in our " clachan " life, indeed, is written at her instigation. At first when she discovered that I had become an author she was contemptuous, and her sneers on the subject made me uncomfortable. About a month ago, however, Janet began to look upon authorship in a new light. There are several persons in the glen whom she never passes, even on the Sabbath, without flinging her head so far back that she can see what is taking place behind her. One of these is Teacher M'Queen, and it has struck Janet that I might make the old dominie more humble if I "showed him up in the newspapers."

" Of which he has great need," Janet frequently reminds me.

" I can show him his errors from the pulpit," I tell her.

" You can," says Janet, " and when you're done he wakes up."

Teacher M'Queen does not sleep in church, but Janet scorns him, and therefore insists that he does. Janet watches the congregation so sharply that she has no time to pay much atten-

tion to the sermon.   When this is pointed out
to her she says :

"I have the minister six days a week, and
so I can surely take my een off him on the
Sabbath."

However, I must leave Janet (whom I seem
to have on the brain) and come to Teacher
M'Queen.   Nevertheless, I would have it first
understood that I mean to sketch the dominie
as I know him, not as he is conceived by Janet.

M'Queen has never been a schoolmaster here
in my time.   It will be six years in June since
I came to the glen, and he had retired on a
pension two years before that.   He was a
teacher in the glen (as he tells me every time
we quarrel about whitewashing the session-
house) "long before I was born," and he is
still so hale that he might venture to add that
he will still be a resident here long after I am
dead.   They say that he and the inspector once
nearly came to blows about a vulgar fraction,
but as a rule, I fancy, he was sly rather than
combative on the days of the examination, and
there are queer stories (told by former pupils)
of what he did behind the inspector's back.
The grand ambition of the inspector was to get

him to retire, which he did, after thinking the
matter over for six years. His great subject of
conversation at the social board had always
been the glories of life in Aberdeen, for he
despised what he called the "stagnation" of
the glen, and would frequently say to our
farmers, or to the smith :

" The like of you can have no notion of the
sublime thoughts that fill the brain of an
educated man. Therefore, what do you mean
by presuming to argue with me ? "

Of course, when he decided to retire on a
pension, the universal opinion was that he would
spend his last days in his beloved Aberdeen. I
believe the glen folk were grieved to think that
he would be known to them no more ; for
though he was and is a cantankerous man, it
is impossible to live for years in intimacy with
any one without discovering some good in him.
The dominie had been an indefatigable teacher,
and had done numerous kind-hearted things,
though not, it must be admitted, in a gracious
manner. A number of his old pupils rallied
round him when he retired, and there was a
social gathering given in his honor at the new
school-house. An English village school could

not, I think, make such a display, for even up
in our little glen boys are ambitious of learning,
and there were three ministers and an advocate
(all former pupils) at the gathering. Several
other pupils, who had risen to what in the glen
is called fame, were unable to be present, but
they sent their good wishes and a subscription
to the present. The present to the dominie
consisted of " a purse and sovereigns," but I
never heard how many sovereigns were in the
purse. Perhaps this is one of the things best
kept dark.

Then when the presentation was over, and
the speeches and the tea run down, nearly the
whole glen shook hands with Teacher M'Queen,
and wished him happy days in Aberdeen.

" Thank you kindly," he replied a score of
times, " but I may see you again before I go, as
I've taken lodgings with the smith for a week.
You see, I have some things to do before I can
start."

So the dominie spoke; but the week went
by, and another week, and then another, and
he was still at the smith's. When questioned
as to when he meant to leave, he continued to
say :

"Oh, in a few days. You see I have some things to do before I can start."

One of the things the dominie had to do was to give up his eldership, and this took a long time. I had the story from my predecessor.

"M'Queen used to come up to the manse," Mr. Marr told me, "and explain that as he was going to Aberdeen, he would have to give up his eldership. Then he would sigh, and say, 'You'll get the session-house whitewashed when I'm away;' and I would reply, 'Well, it needs to be whitewashed, and I could never understand why you were so much opposed to whitewashing it.' 'Ah,' he would answer, 'you see James White and I never got on well, and James was for the whitewashing, and so I was bound to go against it. I'll hardly sleep at nights at Aberdeen, for I'll always be thinking James has got his way.' Then when he rose to go (I always let him out myself, because Janet and he used to put up their backs at each other) I would say, 'So I am to understand that you have resigned your eldership?' and he would answer, 'Well, it must come to that, but I think I'll put off resigning for another week, as I'm not just leaving yet, there being some things I must do before I can start.' "

At the smiddy the dominie spoke for a time of the glories of Aberdeen. He had been born there, and educated at the University, and there was a gleam in his eye when he talked of the old college, and of the smell of the sea. But when he was asked whether he had many friends in Aberdeen now, he became silent, and went out alone. His feet took him in the direction of his old school, a miserable little building that was falling to pieces even before the new school was built. Even to this day it is toward the old school that Teacher M'Queen wanders, and I have heard it said that sometimes as he strides along the path, he forgets that the school is no longer in use, and that his own working days are done. He has been seen stopping short at the doorway of the old school (the door is gone), and looking around him as if for his ragged scholars, or listening for the sound of them at play. Then he looks straight before him for a time, and speaks to himself, after which he returns to the smith's and says that he has decided to set off for Aberdeen on Saturday. But Saturday passes, and still there is something to be done before Teacher M'Queen can start.

I think the dominie had been fully six months in his quarters with the smith before he ceased to talk of going to Aberdeen next week. Then he admitted that the winter was too far advanced.

" The east winds are trying in Aberdeen," he allowed, "and it would scarcely be safe to make the change from here to there in midwinter. But I'll go in spring."

Spring came, and the dominie was still in no hurry to go.

" I'll wait till summer, when the days are long," he said.

Then winter came again.

I suppose he did mean to go to Aberdeen at some time. There is something rather pathetic in this. All his life he had looked forward to returning to Aberdeen, and passing his last years in it. When he was a youth he had no thought, we may be sure, of being a dominie in an insignificant glen during all the working years of his life. He came to the glen strong in the belief that very soon he would get a better place, perhaps in the famous grammar school of Aberdeen itself. Everything he saw

here he compared scornfully to what he had
seen in Aberdeen. He would not allow that
the sun shone here as it did there; and the
Aberdeen people excelled all others. His relatives lived in Aberdeen, but they died before
the dominie had a chance of returning perma-
nently to it. He had a love-story, too, as I suppose all men have, and the scene of it was Aberdeen. I don't know why it came to nothing,
for on that subject the dominie, even in his
loquacious hours, shuts his mouth.

He discovered, but tried to put the discovery
from him as something distasteful, that Aberdeen no longer contained a friend of his. He
might have left the glen for it, but though
many persons in the glen would have seen him
on the coach, there was no one to meet him at
Aberdeen station. All his life he had thought
of Aberdeen as his real home, yet during this
time he was making a new home in the glen.
It would have been death for him to leave us.
In the glen he is somebody, but Aberdeen
buried him decades ago.

So the dominie remains with us, and here he
will end his days. In the glen he is still Teacher
M'Queen, while the present schoolmaster is only

Mr. Rowand. Mr. Marr went the way of all the earth some years ago. but still Teacher M'Queen is an elder in the church, still Janet and he shake their heads at each other, and he is still violent in his opposition to the whitewashing of the session-house.

CHAPTER IV.

THE POST.

When a carriage is going one way along our glen road, and the post's bicycle is coming the other way, there is an anxious moment for the persons in the carriage. They will squeeze their vehicle, if they are wise, into a recess, but even then the bicycle may charge into it, for the post's " machine " is more like a restive horse than a thing of wheels, and, except when there is a brae to climb, it is constantly running away with him. It used to back in the middle of braes and whirl him down the way he had come, much like a canoe trying to ascend a rush of water and giving up the contest when near the top. Now, however, the post is more cautious. When he comes to a brae he jumps (and falls) from his velocipede, as he calls it, and drags it up the hill. When he is tired of dragging, he pushes. It has been noticed of our glen that it is all climbing. The road the post has to go is more likè a switchback railway than anything else, so that he is oftener off his velocipede than on it. To the calm outsider the machine doubles his daily work, yet it is the one thing in this world he is proud of.

He is a lanky man, with hair that the wind blows across his eyes, and his age is uncertain. He thinks he must be sixty, but some in the glen say he is seventy. Every day he has some eighteen miles to walk (or " cycle "), but we do not consider this astounding, there being several men of threescore-and-ten in the glen who can still walk their thirty miles on occasion. One of them, indeed, can even fish after it. However, John had set his heart on a velocipede, and two years ago a subscription was started to enable him to buy a second-hand one. Nearly twelve shillings were gathered in a single evening at the school-house for this purpose, the teacher having got up a concert (at which I read Mr. Stanley's account of how he found Livingstone—though the hit of the evening was made by our comic singer). After the money had been presented to the post, he changed his

mind about the bicycle and bought a fiddle, to
the great indignation of the subscribers. He
showed considerable canniness when taken to
task.

" How have I cheated you ? " he asked the
smith's wife.

" We gave money to let you buy a velocipede,
and you've bought a fiddle.   That's how you've
cheated us."

" No, Mary, you misjudge me.   In the testimonial I got with the siller, it said that the
money was raised in recognition of my long
and valuable services."

" Yes, and to let you buy a velocipede."

" There's not a word about a velocipede."

" Maybe it's called a bi—bicycle, but that's
the same thing."

" It's hardly the same thing, but I assure you
bicycles are no mentioned any more than velocipedes."

" Havers ! did I no hear the testimonial read
out ? "

" You did; and I can repeat it to you by
heart, for often I say it to myself when standing beneath a tree till the rain stops.   The
words you're thinking of are as follows :—

'This gift is raised to enable him to buy something that will make his journeys easier.' "

" And surely that means a velocipede ? "

"I don't see but what it might mean a fiddle.
The roads don't seem so long if you have music
to brighten them."

" Well aware you are that these words were
just put in because the dominie's heart failed
him at the word ' velocipede,' he no being sure
how many s's were in it."

" If that's so," said John, cunningly, " the
blame for buying the fiddle should be charged
to the dominie."

It was apparently only to " stop talk " that the
post by and by began to construct a velocipede
out of his own head. At first he took little
interest in the enterprise, perhaps because he
was hopeless, but soon he became so enamored
of it that he grudged the time spent in delivering letters. My housekeeper wanted me to
have him dismissed promptly (Janet thinks
the Government would not dare to disobey the
orders of a Free Church minister), because one
day he said to her :

" Hie, Janet; there's twa or three letters
for the minister in my bag. You'll better cry

10

in at the smith's for them. They're on the mantelpiece."

"Bring them yourself," said Janet, indignantly.

"I'll try to run up with them," said the audacious post, "before supper time, but I'm terribly busy making my velocipede."

"Are you paid by the Government for making velocipedes," demanded Janet, "or for delivering letters?"

"I disdain to argue with a woman," replied John. "Stand out of the light, woman."

"Woman indeed!" said Janet, holding her head high.

John and the smith are only on speaking terms now when the velocipede is broken, which is once a week or so. Then they mend it between them. Their quarrel arose in this way. John began to make his vehicle in his own kitchen, from which he was driven by his wife to a shed that is cold in winter, because it wants half of the roof. Having made a machine here that looked complete when leaning against the side of the shed, but came to pieces if you tried to sit on it, John had to call in the smith, and for a month, the two men were engaged in the evenings in giving it finishing touches. They were great friends during this period, and, indeed, up to the memorable day when the post's steed was first seen by the glen at large. It was so much admired that John felt it to be his duty to himself and the Postmaster-General to claim full credit for the construction. From the same day the smith took to maintaining that he had made the velocipede.

" The smith lent me some nails and a hammer," John said, " but I made the thing."

" Him make a bicycle ! " said the smith, scornfully. " I let him hold the nails till I needed them, but I did all the work."

" A laddie could have done all the smith did," John explained.

" That's true," retorted the smith, " if a laddie could have made the bicycle."

So fierce did the controversy run that the smith turned his back when John came clattering along on his wooden horse. Nevertheless, both love that bicycle, and when anything is wrong with it they rush for hammers and twine. There is a great deal of twine about the machine, and, when it cuts, the wheels go different ways.

To describe the post's velocipede is altogether beyond my pen. To me it looks like a little cart wheel in chase of a big one, with an excited rider trying to keep them apart.

"The post's coming!" some one says at the "clachan," and then mothers dart into the road for their children to save them from death, while terrified hens run this way and that. Then with a clatter John bears down upon us, shouting :

"Clear the road there."

"Stop him," some one cries to John.

"I canna," says John ; "he's away with me again. Grip him at the back."

Some bold spirit seizes the little wheel, and is dragged along by the infuriated bicycle until John is able to descend.

"Bring me a drink of water," he pants.

But it is not always thus that the post arrives. Sometimes he is hours late, and we say :

"I can't make out why John is so late."

"He'll have broken down," is suggested next.

By and by John walks into the hamlet, pushing his bicycle before him, or laden with various parts of it.

" We've had an accident,"· he explains, as if an explanation were necessary.

Sometimes the post comes to grief as well as his machine, and we have to sally forth to look for him. Once something still more remarkable happened. The bicycle arrived alone. We hurried up the brae, at the foot of which the hamlet lies, and near the top we found John prone in the middle of a wet road.

" Don't bother about me," he cried, " but help me to find the velocipede. It's bolted."

I should say that it would be easier to walk forty miles on our roads than to ride five on that demon machine, but the post by no means agrees with me.

" That velocipede's like a watch," he says, fondly. " So long as I never had one I didn't miss it, but now I couldn't do without it."

CHAPTER V.

A WEDDING IN THE SMIDDY.

I PROMISED to take the world at large into my confidence on the subject of our wedding at the smiddy. You in London, no doubt, dress more gorgeously for marriages than we do—though we can present a fine show of color —and you do not make your own wedding-cake, as Lizzie did. But what is your excitement to ours? I suppose you have many scores of marriages for our one, but you only know of those from the newspapers. "At so-and-so, by the Rev. Mr. Such-a-one, John to Elizabeth, eldest daughter of Thomas." That is all you know of the couple who were married round the corner, and therefore, I say, a hundred such weddings are less eventful in your community than one wedding in ours.

Lizzie is off to Southampton with her husband. As the carriage drove off behind two horses that could with difficulty pull it through the snow, Janet suddenly appeared at my elbow and remarked:

"Well, well, she has him now, and may she have her joy of him."

"Ah, Janet," I said, "you see you were wrong. You said he would never come for her."

"No, no," answered Janet. "I just said Lizzie made too sure about him, seeing as he was at the other side of the world. These sailors are scarce to be trusted."

"But you see this one has turned up a trump."

"That remains to be seen. Anybody that's single can marry a woman, but it's no so easy to keep her comfortable."

I suppose Janet is really glad that the sailor did turn up and claim Lizzie, but she is annoyed in a way too. The fact is that Janet was skeptical about the sailor. I never saw Janet reading anything but the *Free Church Monthly*, yet she must have obtained her wide knowledge of sailors from books. She considers them very bad characters, but is too shrewd to give her reasons.

"We all ken what sailors are," is her dark way of denouncing those who go down to the sea in ships, and then she shakes her head and purses up her mouth as if she could tell things about sailors that would make our hair rise.

I think it was in Glasgow that Lizzie met the sailor—three years ago. She had gone there to be a servant, but the size of the place (according to her father) frightened her, and in a few months she was back at the clachan. We were all quite excited to see her again in the church, and the general impression was that Glasgow had "made her a deal more lady-like." In Janet's opinion she was just a little too lady-like to be natural.

In a week's time there was a wild rumor through the glen that Lizzie was to be married.

"Not she," said Janet, uneasily.

Soon, however, Janet had to admit that there was truth in the story, for "the way Lizzie wandered up the road looking for the post showed she had a man on her mind."

Lizzie, I think, wanted to keep her wonderful secret to herself, but that could not be done.

"I canna sleep at nights for wondering who

Lizzie is to get," Janet admitted to me. So in order to preserve her health Janet studied the affair, reflected (u the kind of people Lizzie was likely to meet in Glasgow, asked Lizzie to the manse to tea (with no result), and then asked Lizzie's mother (victory). Lizzie was to be married to a sailor.

" I'm cheated," said Janet, " if she ever sets eyes on him again. Oh, we all ken what sailors are."

You must not think Janet too spiteful. Marriages were always too much for her, but after the wedding is over she becomes good-natured again. She is a strange mixture, and, I rather think, very romantic, despite her cynical talk.

Well, I confess now that for a time I was somewhat afraid of Lizzie's sailor myself. His letters became few in number, and often I saw Lizzie with red eyes after the post had passed. She had too much work to do to allow her to mope, but she became unhappy and showed a want of spirit that alarmed her father, who liked to shout at his relatives and have them shout back at him.

" I wish she had never set eyes on that

sailor," he said to me one day when Lizzie was troubling him.

" She could have had William Simpson," her mother said to Janet.

" I question that," said Janet, in repeating the remark to me.

But though all the clachan shook its head at the sailor, and repeated Janet's aphorism about sailors as a class, Lizzie refused to believe her lover untrue.

" The only way to get her to flare up at me," her father said, " is to say a word against her lad. She will not stand that."

And, after all, we were wrong and Lizzie was right. In the beginning of the winter Janet walked into my study and parlor (she never knocks), and said ·

"He's come ! "

" Who ? " I asked.

" The sailor. Lizzie's sailor. It's a perfect disgrace."

" Hoots, Janet, it's the very reverse. I'm delighted ; and so, I suppose, are you in your heart."

" I'm not grudging her the man if she wants him," said Janet, flinging up her head, " but

the disgrace is in the public way he marched
past me with his arm round her.   It affronted
me."

Janet gave me details.   She had been to a
farm for the milk and passed Lizzie, who had
wandered out to meet the post as usual.

" I've no letter for ye, Lizzie," the post said,
and Lizzie sighed.

" No, my lass," the post continued, " but
I've something better."

Lizzie was wondering what it could be, when
a man jumped out from behind a hedge, at the
sight of whom Lizzie screamed with joy.   It
was her sailor.

" I would never have let on I was so fond of
him," said Janet.

" But did he not seem fond of her ? " I
asked.

" That was the disgrace," said Janet.   " He
marched off to her father's house with his arm
round her ; yes, passed me and a wheen other
folk, and looked as if he neither kent nor cared
how public he was making himself.   She did
not care either."

I addressed some remarks to Janet on the
subject of meddling with other people's affairs,

pointing out that she was now half an hour late with my tea; but I, too, was interested to see the sailor. I shall never forget what a change had come over Lizzie when I saw her next. The life was back in her face, she bustled about the house as busy as a bee, and her walk was springy.

"This is him," she said to me, and then the sailor came forward and grinned. He was usually grinning when I saw him, but he had an honest, open face, if a very youthful one.

The sailor stayed on at the clachan till the marriage, and continued to scandalize Janet by strutting "past the very manse gate" with his arm round the happy Lizzie.

"He has no notion of the solemnity of marriage," Janet informed me, "or he would look less jolly. I would not like a man that joked about his marriage."

The sailor undoubtedly did joke. He seemed to look on the coming event as the most comical affair in the world's history, and when he spoke of it he slapped his knees and roared. But there was daily fresh evidence that he was devoted to Lizzie.

The wedding took place in the smiddy,

because it is a big place, and all the glen was invited. Lizzie would have had the company comparatively select, but the sailor asked every one to come whom he fell in with, and he had few refusals. He was wonderfully "flush" of money, too, and had not Lizzie taken control of it, would have given it all away before the marriage took place.

"It's a mercy Lizzie kens the worth of a bawbee," her mother said, "for he would scatter his siller among the very bairns as if it was corn and he was feeding hens."

All the chairs in the five houses were not sufficient to seat the guests, but the smith is a handy man, and he made forms by crossing planks on tubs. The smiddy was an amazing sight, lit up with two big lamps, and the bride, let me inform those who tend to scoff, was dressed in white. As for the sailor, we have perhaps never had so showily dressed a gentleman in our parts. For this occasion he discarded his seafaring "rig-out" (as he called it), and appeared resplendent in a black frock coat (tight at the neck), a light blue waistcoat (richly ornamented), and gray trousers with a green stripe. His boots were new and so genteel that as the evening wore on he had to kick them off and dance in his stocking soles.

Janet tells me that Lizzie had gone through the ceremony in private with her sailor a number of times, so that he might make no mistake. The smith, asked to take my place at these rehearsals, declined on the ground that he forgot how the knot was tied; but his wife had a better memory, and I understand that she even mimicked me—for which I must take her to task one of these days.

However, despite all these precautions, the sailor was a little demonstrative during the ceremony, and slipped his arm round the bride "to steady her." Janet wonders that Lizzie did not fling his arms from her, but Lizzie was too nervous now to know what her swain was about.

Then came the supper and the songs and the speeches. The tourists who picture us shivering, silent, and depressed all through the winter should have been in the smiddy that night.

I proposed the health of the young couple, and when I called Lizzie by her new name, "Mrs. Fairweather," the sailor flung back his head and roared with glee till he choked, and Lizzie's first duty as a wife was to hit him hard between the shoulder blades. When he was sufficiently composed to reply, he rose to his feet and grinned round the room.

" Mrs. Fairweather," he cried in an ecstasy of delight and again choked.

The smith induced him to make another attempt, and this time he got as far as " Ladies and gentlemen, me and my wife—" when the speech ended prematurely in resounding chuckles. The last we saw of him, when the carriage drove away, he was still grinning ; but that, as he explained, was because " he had got Lizzie at last." " You'll be a good husband to her, I hope," I said.

" Will I not ! " he cried, and his arm went round his wife again.

DITE DEUCHARS.

Wonderful is the variety of pleasures in Thrums. One has no sooner unyoked from his loom than something exhilarating happens. In the same hour I have known a barn go on fire in the Marywellbrae, a merriment caravan stick on the Brig of the Kelpies, and a lord dine in the Quharity Arms parlor, the view of which is commanded from the top of Hookey Crewe's dyke. To see everything worth seeing is impossible, simply because the days are not thirty-six hours long. Most of us, however, see our fill, Dite Deuchars being the strange exception.

A bad boy had flung a good boy's bonnet on to Haggart's roof, and we had gone for it with a ladder. We were now sitting up there,

to see what it was like. Conversation had
languished, but Haggart said " Ay," and then
again " Umpha," as one may shove a piece of
paper into a dying fire to make a momentary
blaze. In the yard the boys were now map-
ping out the "Pilgrim's Progress" with kail-
runts. Women were sitting on dykes, knit-
ting stockings. Snecky Hobart was pitting
his potatoes. We could join him presently if
Haggart refused to add to our stock of information ; but the humorist was sucking in his lips,
and then blowing them out—and we knew
what that meant. To look at his mouth re-
hearsing was to be suddenly hungry. We had
planted ourselves more firmly on the roof
when—

" Wha's killing ? " cried Lunan.

The screech and skirl of a pig under the
knife had suddenly shaken Thrums.

" Lookaboutyou's killing," cried Dite turning
hastily to the ladder.

There followed a rush of feet along the
Tenements. Snecky Hobart flung down his
spade, the two laddies plucked up the Slough
of Despond, and were off before him. The
women fell off the dykes as if shot.

11

" You're coming, Tammas, surely ? " said Dite, already on the ladder.

" Not me," answered Haggart. " If Lookaboutyou likes to kill without telling me aforehand, I dinna gang near him."

" Come awa', Davit," said Dite to Lunan.

"I dinna deny," said Lunan, " but what my feet's tickly to start; but this I will say, that it was as little as Lookaboutyou could have done to tell Tammas Haggart he was killing."

" But Tammas hadna speired ? "

"Speir!" cried Haggart. " Let me tell you, Dite Deuchars, a humorist doesna speir ; he just answers. But awa' wi' you to the farm; and tell Lookaboutyou that if he thinks I'm angered at his no telling me he was killing, he was never mair mista'en."

" I wouldna leave you," said Dite, " if you had been on your adventures, but you're no, and I'm so unlucky, I hardly ever see ony oncommon thing."

" On my adventures I'll be in a minute, for the screaming o' that swine calls to my mind an extraordinar' meeting I had wi' a coachfu' o' pirates."

"Sal, I would like to hear that," said Dite, stepping on to the roof again.

The squeals of the pig broke out afresh.

"That's mair than I can stand," cried Dite sliding down the ladder. He ran a few yards, and then turned back undecidedly.

"Is it a partickler wonderful adventure, Tammas?" we heard him cry, though we could not see him.

Haggart put his underlip firmly over the upper one.

"You micht tell me, Tammas," cried the voice.

It was not for us to speak, and Haggart would not.

"I canna make up my mind," Dite continued, sadly, "whether to bide wi' you, or to gang to the killing. If I dinna gang, I'm sure to wish I had ga'en; and if I gang, I'll think the hale time about what I'm missing."

We heard him sigh, and then the clatter of his heels.

"He's a lang time, though," said Lunan, "in turning the close. We should see him when he gets that length."

"The onlucky crittur 'll be wavering in the

close," said Haggart, "no able to make up his mind whether to gang on or turn back. I tell you, lads, to have twa minds is as confusing as twins."

We saw Dite reach the mouth of the close, where he stopped and looked longingly at us. Then he ran on, then he stopped again, then he turned back.

"He's coming back, after all," said Lunan.

"Ou, he'll be off again directly," Haggart said, with acumen, as we discoursed the next minute. "Ay, the body's as ondecided as a bairn standing wi' a bawbee in its hand, looking in at the window o' a sweetie shop."

We saw Dite take the backwynd like one who had at last forgotten our counter-attractions, but just as he was finally disappearing from view he ran into a group of women.

"Tod, he's coming back again," said Lunan, breaking into the middle of Haggart's story. "No wonder the crittur's onlucky!"

Dite, however, only came back a little way. He then climbed the glebe dyke, and hurried off up the park.

"He's fair demented," said Lunan, "for that's as little the road to Lookaboutyou's as it's the road to the tap o' this hoose."

The women sauntered nearer, and when they were within earshot Haggart stopped his narrative to shout—

"Susie Linn, what made Dite Deuchars take the glebe park?"

"He's awa' to see Easie Pennycuick's new crutches," replied Susie. "The pridefu' stock has got a pair that cost twal and saxpence (so she says), and she's inviting a'body in to see them."

"The wy she's lifted up about these crutches," broke in Haggart's wife, Chirsty, from her window, "is hard to bear; and I ken I'll no gang to look at them. 'Have you seen my new crutches?' she says, as soon as her een lichts on you."

"That's true, Chirsty, and she came in the kirk late wi' them last Sabbath of set purpose. Weel, we telt Dite about them in the backwynd, and he's awa' to see them. He said—— If that's no him coming back!"

Dite had turned, and was hastening down the field.

"He's changed his mind again," said Lunan. "He's off to the killing, after all."

"Hoy, Dite Deuchars," shouted Susie Linn.

Dite hesitated, looking first in the direction of Lookaboutyou's, and then at us.

"He's coming here," said one of the women.

"He's halted," said another.

"He's awa' to the killing at Lookaboutyou's," cried Susie Linn.

"As sure as death he's climbing into the glebe park again," said Lunan. "Oh, the onlucky body!"

"We maun turn our backs to the distracted crittur," said Haggart, "or I'll never finish my adventure."

It was a marvelous adventure, with as many morals as Dite had minds; and when we had talked it over, as well as listened to it, we prepared to descend the ladder.

"Ca' canny," cried Haggart, "there's somebody coming up."

Dite Deuchars, flushed with running, appeared at the top of the ladder.

"Was it a big swine?" asked Lunan.

"I didna gang to the killing. I heard that Easie Pennycuick——"

" Ay, and what thocht you of her crutches ? "

" Truth to tell, Davit, I didna see them, for I couldna make up my mind whether to gang to Easie's or to Lookaboutyou's. They were both so enticing that in the tail o' the day I sat down on the glebe dyke, despising mysel' michty."

" And a despiseable figure you maun have been."

" Ay, but I've come back to hear your adventure, Tammas."

" The adventure's finished," replied Haggart, " and we're coming down."

Dite tottered off the ladder.

" Dagont ! " he cried.

" Let this be a warning to you," said Haggart, " that them that's greedy for a'thing gets naething."

Dite, however, was looking so mournful that the very bucket on which he sat down might have been sorry for him.

" Dinna tell me I'm an ill-gittit man," he said, dejectedly, " for I'm no. A'thing 's agin me. I'm keener to see curious oncommon things than ony ane o' ye, but do I see them? The day the doctor's shalt flung him in the school-wynd, whaur was I? Oh, wi' my usual luck, of course, I had gone round by the banker's close. On the hill, market day, I sat in the quarry for an hour, and naething happened. Syne I taks a dander through the wood, and no suner am I out o' sicht than a ga'en-about body flings himsel' ower the quarry. Jeames McQuhatty and Pete Dundas saw him, though they hadna been there a quarter as lang as me. Sax month on end I'm as reg'lar at the kirk as if I got my living out o' the minister, and naething wonderful occurs; but one single Sabbath I taks to my bed, and behold! in the afternoon the minister swounds dead awa' in the pulpit. When the show took fire in the square, was I there? Na, na, you may be sure I had been sent out o' the wy to the fishing. Did I see Sam'l Robb fall off his hoose? Not me, though we had been neighbors for a twalmonth. What was the name o' the only man in the east town end that sleepit through the nicht o' the Weavers' Riot and never woke up till it was a' ower? The name o' that man was Dite Deuchars."

"Lad, lad, you're onlucky; but I didna ken you had brooded on't like this."

" I've brooded on't till I'm a gey queer character. Tammas Haggart, let me speir this at you. Afore you met the pirate coach, did you or did you no come to a cross-road ? "

" Man, Dite, I mind I did ; but how did you ken ? "

" Ken ! I guessed it. I tell you, if I had been in your place, as sure as luck's agin me, I would ha'e ta'en the other road, and never fallen in wi' the pirates ava. That's what it is to be an onlucky man. Tammas Haggart——"

" Ay, Dite ? "

" There's few things you dinna see humor in, but I think I ken one that beats you."

" Namely, yoursel', Dite ? "

" Namely, mysel'."

" No, Dite," Haggart said, thoughtfully, " I admit I see no humor in you. Ay, you're a melancholy case. You had better gang awa' to your bed."

" Sic an onlucky man as me," replied Dite, doggedly, " doesna deserve a bed. I'm ga'en to sit for an hour on this bucket and sneer at mysel'."

THE MINISTER'S GOWN.

On the morning after a probationer has been chosen minister of a church, his landlady intimates through the key-hole of his bedroom that a gentleman has called " about the gown." The gentleman is from a firm that supplies gowns, and he has arrived early to forestall the representative of another firm. About the same time, two ladies (in black jackets) begin to collect from the other ladies of the congregation the money which is to pay for the gown, and by and by it is presented to the chosen of the people at a soirée. Such is the natural history of the minister's gown.

But congregations there be ("by steamer to Inverary, thence hire ") that love not gowns, and it was one of these that " called " Findlater, M.A., a short year ago. Never until this had

there been a gown in their pulpit, nor did the
Session think that innovations should come with
Findlater. The ladies of the congregation,
however (of whom one had a sealskin coat, and
therefore was not to be slighted), "gathered"
a gown, and Findlater swore to wear it: and
worn it he has every Sunday since, except when
it is not there to wear. For the whereabouts of
that gown is only known at irregular intervals
to many persons at a time. Now it is in the
lawful owner's possession, and again in the
hands of the enemy—that is, of the Session—
who scruple not to make off with it of a Saturday night and restore it to the vestry on Monday morning.

Lest it be concluded that the gown has bred
ill-feeling between the pastor and his people,
let me say at once that this is not so. It has
been admitted by all (though neither in writing
nor in spoken words) that, gown or no gown,
Findlater is the man for them. True, a maiden
who subscribed has been asked to return a ring
by a gentleman who, though not a deacon, has
already the walk of one; but this she refused
to do on the ground that men are hard to get;
and thus a tragedy was averted. Again, though

the opposition is, undeniably, led by the pillars
of the Kirk, the gown was presented by her of
the sealskin, who was educated at an Edinburgh
boarding-school where only Free Church plants
are received; and thus must her actions be right
and proper.   It is, then, with a chastened ex-
ultation that the Session see the minister fail
to find his gown; while on those occasions
when he unexpectedly appears in it (they thinking it to be at that moment hidden in the
smiddy), they good-naturedly overlook the triumph with which he gives out his first psalm.

How often the gown has disappeared and
been returned or captured I cannot tell.   Only
occasionally am I in the place for a week-end,
and then can no one assure me for certain
whether or no we are to have a gown Sunday.
At first the gown was kept in the vestry, where
it hung on a nail so temptingly that a garden-
rake entered by the window and abducted it.
That was on a Saturday evening, and service
on the following day began some twenty minutes late.   The gown was on its nail by Monday at 10 A. M., and locked away in the vestry-
press at 11 A. M.; and for some weeks the minister triumphed.   Then again had he to preach

without his gown in the forenoon. Between
services it was discovered lurking behind a
tombstone. Some say that he had left the key
in the press : others that, whether locked or
not, the press opens if shaken by those who
have the knack of it. But those supposed to
have the knack of it say nothing, and equally
reticent is Findlater, save in the presence of
Kirsteen, his housekeeper, who can goad any
man to language.

Latterly Findlater has kept the gown in the
manse, from which he now walks to church in
it. Even from the manse has it been removed
by daring hands, despite (as the minister once
thought) Kirsteen's unwearying guard over it,
but (as he now holds) with the connivance of
that double woman. There was a time when
Kirsteen was allowed to take the gown to the
kitchen, there to renew the seams at the arm-
pit, which give way when Findlater is pro-
nouncing the benediction ; but then had the
gown a habit of running off through the shrub-
bery the moment her back was turned. Hence
the new regulation that, when the gown re-
quires mending, it is mended in the minister's
presence.

The lady in the sealskin (which the envious call plush, though they sit immediately behind her, and have felt it with their fingers, when pretending to be merely laying their Bible on the " board ") considers Findlater's silence in the face of such persecution singularly beautiful; and so it is, unless Kirsteen's stories be true of the way he opens out on the subject to her. Only once in public has the gown led to his forgetting himself: and then the circumstances were trying. The manse garden and the church were only the breadth of a burn and a high-road apart, and the minister has to jump the burn. I have seen him do so often, and always first with a look round to apologize for the undignified nature of the act. Such, I am sure, is his meaning ; but there are those who maintain that he only looks about him to make sure that no one is in the vicinity with designs on the gown. On the occasion in question, just as he was on the point of jumping, it seemed to him that an impious hand had tried to pluck the gown off him. His assailant was in reality but the branch of a tree dipping suddenly in the wind till it touched his shoulder; but before Findlater realized this he clutched his gown with both hands and—said something.

I called at the manse to-day and found Findlater in his study, busy at his sermon. He was sitting on the gown.

THE CAPTAIN OF THE SCHOOL.

WHEN Peterkin, who is twelve, wrote to us that there was a possibility ("but don't count on it," he said) of his bringing the captain of the school home with him for a holiday, we had little conception what it meant. The captain we only knew by report as the "man" who lifted leg-balls over the pavilion and was said to have made a joke to the head-master's wife. By and by we understood the distinction that was to be conferred on us. Peterkin instructed his mother to send the captain a formal invitation addressed "J. Rawlins, Esq." This was done, but in such a way that Peterkin feared we might lose our distinguished visitor. "You shouldn't have asked him for all the holidays," Peterkin wrote, "as he has promised a heap of fellows." Then came a condescending note from the captain, saying that if he could manage it he would give us a few days. In this letter he referred to Peterkin as his young friend. Peterkin wrote shortly afterwards asking his sister Grizel to send him her photograph. " If you haven't one," he added, " what is the color of your eyes ? " Grizel is eighteen, which is also, I believe, the age of J. Rawlins. We concluded that the captain had been sounding Peterkin about the attractions that our home could offer him ; but Grizel neither sent her brother a photograph nor any account of her personal appearance. " It doesn't matter," Peterkin wrote back; " I told him you were dark." Grizel is rather fair, but Peterkin had not noticed that.

Up to the very last he was in an agony lest the captain should disappoint him. " Don't tell anybody he is coming," he advised us, " for of course there is no saying what may turn up." Nevertheless the captain came, and we sent the dog-cart to the station to meet him and Peterkin. On all previous occasions one of us had gone to the station with the cart ; but Peterkin wrote asking us not to do so this time. " Rawlins hates any fuss," he said.

Somewhat to our relief, we found the captain more modest than it would have been reasonable to expect. " This is Rawlins," was Peterkin's simple introduction ; but it could not have been done with more pride had the guest been Mr. W. G. Grace himself. One thing I liked in Rawlins from the first : his consideration for others. When Peterkin's mother and sister embraced that boy on the doorstep, Rawlins pretended not to see. Peterkin frowned, however, at this show of affection, and with a red face looked at the captain to see how he took it. With much good taste, Peterkin said nothing about this " fuss " on the door-step, and I concluded that he would let it slide. It has so far been a characteristic of that boy that he can let anything which is disagreeable escape his memory. This time, however, as I subsequently learned, he had only bottled up his wrath to pour it out upon his sister. Finding her alone in the course of the day, he opened his mind by remarking that this was a nice sort of thing she had done, making a fool of him before another fellow. Asked boldly—for Grizel can be freezing on occasion not only to her own brother, but to other people's brothers

—what he meant, Peterkin inquired hotly if she was going to pretend that she had not kissed him in Rawlins' presence. Grizel replied that if Rawlins thought anything of that he was a nasty boy; at which Peterkin echoed " boy " with a grim laugh, and said he only hoped she would see the captain some day when the ground suited his style of bowling. Grizel replied contemptuously that the time would come when both Peterkin and his disagreeable friend would be glad to be kissed; upon which her brother flung out of the room, warmly protesting that she had no right to bring such charges against fellows.

Though Grizel was thus a little prejudiced against the captain, he had not been a day in the house when we began to feel the honor that his visit conferred on us. He was modest almost to the verge of shyness; but it was the modesty that is worn by a man who knows he can afford it. While Peterkin was there Rawlins had no need to boast, for Peterkin did the boasting for him. When, however, the captain exerted himself to talk, Peterkin was contented to retire into the shade and gaze at him. He would look at all of us from his seat

in the background, and note how Rawlins was
striking us. Peterkin's face as he gazed upon
that of the captain went far beyond the rapture of a lover singing to his mistress's eye-
brow. He fetched and carried for him, antici-
pated his wants as if Rawlins were an invalid,
and bore his rebukes meekly. When Rawlins
thought that Peterkin was speaking too much,
he had merely to tell him to shut up, when
Peterkin instantly collapsed. We noticed one
great change in Peterkin. Formerly, when he
came home for the holidays he had strongly
objected to making what he called drawing-
room calls, but all that was changed. Now he
went from house to house showing the captain
off. "This is Rawlins," remained his favorite
form of introduction. He is a boy who can
never feel comfortable in a drawing-room, and
so the visits were generally of short duration.
They had to go because they were due in
another house in a quarter of an hour, or he
had promised to let Jemmy Clinker (who is
our local cobbler and a great cricketer) see
Rawlins. When a lady engaged the captain
in conversation, Peterkin did not scruple to
sign to her not to bother him too much; and

if they were asked to call again, Peterkin said he couldn't promise. There was a remarkable thing the captain could do to a walking stick, which Peterkin wanted him to do everywhere. It consisted in lying flat on the floor, and then raising yourself in an extraordinary way by means of the stick. I believe it is a very difficult feat, and the only time I saw our guest prevailed upon to perform it he looked rather apoplectic. Sometimes he would not do it, apparently because he was not certain whether it was a dignified proceeding. He found it very hard, nevertheless, to resist the temptation, and it was the glory of Peterkin to see him yield to it. From certain noises heard in Peterkin's bedroom it is believed that he is practicing the feat himself.

Peterkin, you must be told, is an affectionate boy, and almost demonstrative to his relatives if no one is looking. He was consequently very anxious to know what the captain thought of us all, and brought us our testimonials as proudly as if they were medals awarded for saving life at sea. It is pleasant to me to know that I am the kind of governor Rawlins would have liked himself, had he required one.

Peterkin's mother, however, is the captain's favorite. She pretended to take the young man's preference as a joke when her son informed her of it, but in reality I am sure she felt greatly relieved. If Rawlins had objected to us, it would have put Peterkin in a very awkward position. As for Grizel, the captain thinks her a very nice little girl, but "for choice," he says (according to Peterkin), "give him a bigger woman." Grizel was greatly annoyed when he told her this, which much surprised him, for he thought it quite as much as she had any right to expect. On the whole we were perhaps rather glad when Rawlins left, for it was somewhat trying to live up to him. Peterkin's mother, too, has discovered that her boy has become round-shouldered. It is believed that this is the result of a habit he acquired when in Rawlins' company of leaning forward to catch what people were saying about the captain.

A POWERFUL DRUG.

(NO HOUSEHOLD SHOULD BE WITHOUT IT.)

ALL respectable chemists, Montgomery assures me, keep the cio-root. That is the name of the drug, and Montgomery is the man who ought to write its testimonials. This is a testimonial to the efficacy of the cio-root, and I write it the more willingly because, until the case of Montgomery cropped up, I had no faith in patent medicines. Seeing, however, is, they say, believing; and I have seen what the cio-root did for Montgomery. I can well believe now that it can do anything, from removing grease-spots to making your child cry out in the night.

Montgomery, who was married years ago, is subject to headaches, and formerly his only way of treating them was to lie in bed and read a light novel. By the time the novel was finished, so, as a rule, was the headache. This treatment rather interfered with his work, however, and he tried various medicines which were guaranteed to cure rapidly. None of them had the least result, until one day, some two months ago, good fortune made him run against an old friend in Chambers Street. Montgomery, having a headache, mentioned it, and his friend asked him if he had tried the cio-root. The name even was unfamiliar to Montgomery, but his friend spoke so enthusiastically of it that the headache man took a note of it. He was told that it had never been known to fail, and the particular merit of it was that it drove the headache away in five minutes. The proper dose to take was half an inch of the root, which was to be sucked and eventually swallowed. Montgomery tried several chemists in vain, for they had not heard of it, but at last he got it on George IV. Bridge. He had so often carried home in triumph a "certain cure," which was subsequently flung out of the window in disgust, that his wife shook her head at the cio-root, and advised him not to be too hopeful. However, the cio-root surpassed the fondest expectations. It completely cured Montgomery in less than the five minutes. Several times he tried it, and always with the same triumphant result. Having at last got a drug to make an idol of, it is not perhaps to be wondered at that Montgomery was full of gratitude. He kept a three-pound tin of the cio-root on his library-table, and the moment he felt a headache coming on he said, " Excuse me for one moment," and bit off half an inch of cio-root.

The headaches never had a chance. It was therefore natural, though none the less annoying, that his one topic of conversation should become the properties of this remarkable drug. You would drop in on him, glowing over the prospect of a delightful two hours' wrangle over the crofter question, but he pushed the subject away with a wave of his hand, and begged to introduce to our notice the cio-root. Sitting there smoking, his somewhat dull countenance would suddenly light up as his eyes came to rest on the three-pound tin. He was always advising us to try the cio-root, and when we said we did not have a headache he got sulky. The first thing he asked us when we met was whether we had a headache, and often he clipped

off an inch or two of the cio-root and gave it us
in a piece of paper, so that the headache might
not take us unawares. I believe he rather enjoyed waking with a headache, for he knew that
it would not have a chance. If his wife had
been a jealous woman, she would not have liked
the way he talked of the cio-root.

Some of us did try the drug, either to please
him or because we were really curious about it.
Whatever the reason, none of us, I think, were
prejudiced. We tested it on its merits, and
came unanimously to the conclusion that they
were negative. The cio-root did us no harm.
The taste was what one may imagine to be the
taste of the root of any rotten tree dipped in
tar, which was subsequently allowed to dry.
As we were all of one mind on the subject, we
insisted with Montgomery that the cio-root was
a fraud. Frequently we had such altercations
with him on the subject that we parted in sneers,
and ultimately we said that it would be best not
to goad him too far; so we arranged merely to
chaff him about his faith in the root, and never
went farther than insisting, in a pleasant way,
that he was cured, not by the cio-root, but by
his believing in it. Montgomery rejected this

theory with indignation, but we stuck to it and never doubted it. Events, nevertheless, will show you that Montgomery was right and that we were wrong.

The triumph of cio-root came as recently as yesterday. Montgomery, his wife, and myself had arranged to go into Glasgow for the day. I called for them in the forenoon and had to wait, as Montgomery had gone along to the office to see if there were any letters. He arrived soon after me, saying that he had a headache, but saying it in a cheery way, for he knew that the root was in the next room. He disappeared into the library to nibble half an inch of the cio-root, and shortly afterwards we set off. The headache had been dispelled as usual. In the train he and I had another argument about the one great drug, and he ridiculed my notion about its being faith that drove his headache away. I may hurry over the next two hours, up to the time when we wandered into Buchanan Street. There Montgomery met a friend, to whom he introduced me. The gentleman was in a hurry, so we only spoke for a moment, but after he had left us he turned back.

" Montgomery," he said, " do you remember

that day I met you in Chambers Street, Edinburgh?"

"I have good reason for remembering the occasion," said Montgomery, meaning to begin the story of his wonderful cure; but his friend, who had to catch a 'bus, cut him short.

"I told you at that time," he said, "about a new drug called the cio-root, which had a great reputation for curing headaches."

"Yes," said Montgomery; "I always wanted to thank you——"

His friend, however, broke in again—

"I have been troubled in my mind since then," he said, "because I was told afterwards that I had made a mistake about the proper dose. If you try the cio-root, don't take half an inch, as I recommended, but a quarter of an inch. Don't forget. It is of vital importance."

Then he jumped into his 'bus, but I called after him, "What would be the effect of half an inch?"

"Certain death," he shouted back, and was gone. I turned to look at Montgomery and his wife. She let her umbrella fall and he had turned white. "Of course there is nothing to be alarmed about," I said, in a reassuring way. " Montgomery has taken half an inch scores of times; you say it always cured you ? "

" Yes, yes," Montgomery answered; but his voice sounded hollow.

Up to this point the snow had kept off, but now it began to fall in a soaking drizzle. If you are superstitious you can take this as an omen. For the rest of the day, certainly, we had a miserable time of it. I had to do all the talking, and while I laughed and jested, I noticed that Mrs. Montgomery was looking anxiously from time to time at her husband. She was afraid to ask him if he felt unwell, and he kept up, not wanting to alarm her. But he walked like a man who knew that he had come to his last page. At my suggestion we went to St. Enoch's Station Hotel to have dinner. I had dinner, Mrs. Montgomery pretended to have dinner, but Montgomery himself did not even make the pretence. He sat with his elbows on the table and his face buried in his hands. At last he said with a groan that he was feeling very ill. He looked so doleful that his wife began to cry.

Montgomery admitted that he blamed the cio-root for his sufferings. He had taken an overdose of it, he said, tragically, and must abide the consequences. I could have shaken him, for reasoning was quite flung away on him. Of course, I repeated what I had said previously about an overdose having done him no harm before, but he only shook his head sadly. I said that his behavior now proved my contention that he only believed in the cio-root because he was told that it had wonderful properties; otherwise he would have laughed at what his friend had just told him. Undoubtedly, I said, his sufferings to-day were purely imaginary. Montgomery did not have sufficient spirits to argue with me, but he murmured in a die-away voice that he had felt strange symptoms ever since we set out from Edinburgh. Now, this was as absurd as anything in Euclid, for he had been boasting of the wonderful cure the drug had effected again, most of the way between Edinburgh and Glasgow. He insisted that he had a splitting headache, and that he was very sick. In the end, as his wife was now in a frenzy, I sent out for a doctor. The doctor came, said " Yes " and "Quite so" to himself, and pronounced Montgomery feverish. That he was feverish by this time, I do not question. He had worked himself into a fever. There was some talk of putting him to bed in the hotel, but he insisted on going home. Though he did not put it so plainly, he gave us to understand that he wanted to die in his own bed.

Never was there a more miserable trio than we in a railway carriage. We got a compartment to ourselves, for, though several passengers opened the door to come in, they shrank back as soon as they saw Montgomery's ghastly face. He lay in a corner of the carriage, with his head done up in flannel, procured at the hotel. He had the rugs and my great-coat over his legs, but he shivered despite them, and when he spoke at all, except to say that he was feeling worse every minute, it was to talk of men cut off in their prime and widows left destitute. At Mrs. Montgomery's wish I telegraphed, from a station at which the train stopped, to the family doctor in Edinburgh, asking him to meet us at the house. He did so; indeed, he was on the steps to help Montgomery up them. We took an arm of

13

the invalid apiece, and dragged him into the library.

It was a fortunate thing that we went into the library, for the first thing Montgomery saw on the table was the half-inch of cio-root which he thought had killed him. He had forgotten to take it.

In ten minutes he was all right. Just as we were sitting down to supper, we heard a cat squalling outside. Montgomery flung a three-pound tin of the cio-root at it.

EVERY MAN HIS OWN DOCTOR.

STATISTICS showing the number of persons who yearly meet their death in our great cities by the fall of telegraph wires are published from time to time. As our cities grow, and the need of telegraphic communication is more generally felt, this danger will become even more conspicuous. Persons who value their lives are earnestly advised not to walk under telegraph wires.

Is it generally realized that every day at least one fatal accident occurs in our streets? So many of these take place at crossings that we would strongly urge the public never to venture across a busy street until all the vehicles have passed.

We find prevalent among our readers an impression that country life is comparatively safe. This mistake has cost Great Britain many lives. The country is so full of hidden dangers that one may be said to risk his health every time he ventures into it.

We feel it our duty to remind holiday-makers that when in the country in the open air, they should never sit down. Many a man, aye, and woman too, has been done to death by neglecting this simple precaution. The recklessness of the public, indeed, in such matters is incomprehensible. The day is hot, they see an inviting grassy bank, and down they sit. Need we repeat that despite the sun (which is ever treacherous) they should continue walking at a smart pace? Yes, bitter experience has taught us that we must repeat such warnings.

When walking in the country holiday-makers should avoid over-heating themselves. Nothing is so conducive to disease. We have no hesitation in saying that nine-tenths of the colds that prove fatal are caught through neglect of this simple rule.

Beware of walking on grass. Though it may be dry to the touch, damp is ever present, and cold caught in this way is always difficult to cure.

Avoid high roads in the country. They are, for the most part, unsheltered, and on hot days the sun beats upon them unmercifully. The perspiration that ensues is the beginning of many a troublesome illness.

Country lanes are stuffy and unhealthy, owing to the sun not getting free ingress into them. They should, therefore, be avoided by all who value their health.

In a magazine we observe an article extolling the pleasures of walking in a wood. That walking in a wood may be pleasant we do not deny, but for our own part we avoid woods. More draughty places could not well be imagined, and many a person who has walked in a wood has had cause to repent it for the rest of his life.

It is every doctor's experience that there is a large public which breaks down in health simply because it does not take sufficient exercise in the open air. Once more we would remind our readers that every man, woman, or child who does not spend at least two hours daily in the open air is slowly committing suicide.

How pitiful it is to hear a business man say, as business men so often say: "Really I cannot take a holiday this summer, my business ties me so to my desk, and, besides, I am feeling quite well. No, I shall send my wife and children to the seaside, and content myself with a Saturday-to-Monday now and again." We solemnly warn all such foolish persons that they are digging their own graves. Change is absolutely essential to health.

Asked the other day why coughs were so prevalent in the autumn, we replied without hesitation, "Because during the past month or two so many persons have changed their beds." City people rush to the seaside in their thousands, and here is the result. A change of beds is dangerous to all, but perhaps chiefly to persons of middle age. We have so often warned the public of this that we can only add now, "If they continue to disregard our warning, their blood be on their own heads." This we say not in anger, but in sorrow.

A case has come to our knowledge of a penny causing death. It had passed through the hands of a person suffering from infectious fever into those of a child, who got it as change from a shop. The child took fever and died in about a fortnight. We would not have mentioned this case had we not known it to be but an instance of what is happening daily. Infection is frequently spread by money, and we would strongly urge no one to take change (especially coppers), from another without seeing it first dipped in warm water. Who can tell where the penny he gets in change from the newspaper-boy has come from?

If ladies, who are ever purchasing new clothes, were aware that disease often lurks in these, they would be less anxious to enter dressmakers' shops. The saleswoman who "fits" them may come daily from a home where her sister lies sick of a fever, or the dress may have been made in some East End den, where infection is rampant. Cases of the kind frequently come to our knowledge, and we would warn the public against this danger that is ever present among us.

Must we again enter a protest against insufficient clothing? We never take a walk along any of our fashionable thoroughfares without seeing scores of persons, especially ladies, insufficiently clad. The same spectacle, alas! may be witnessed in the East End, but for a different reason. Fashionable ladies have a horror of seeming stout, and to retain a slim appearance they will suffer agonies of cold. The world would be appalled if it knew how many of these women die before their fortieth year.

We dress far too heavily. The fact is, that we would be a much healthier people if we wore less clothing. Ladies, especially, wrap themselves up too much, with the result that their blood does not circulate freely. Coats, ulsters, and other wraps cause far more colds than they prevent.

Why have our ladies not the smattering of scientific knowledge that would tell them to vary the thickness of their clothing with the weather? New garments, indeed, they do don for winter, but how many of them put on extra flannels?

We are far too frightened of the weather, treating it as our enemy when it is ready to be our friend. With the first appearance of frost we fly to extra flannel, and thus dangerously overheat ourselves.

Though there has been a great improvement in this matter in recent years, it would be idle to pretend that we are yet a cleanly nation. To speak bluntly, we do not change our under-garments with sufficient frequency. This may be owing to various reasons, but none of them is an excuse. Frequent change of underclothing is a necessity for the preservation of health, and woe to those who neglect this simple precaution.

Owing to the carelessness of servants and others, it is not going too far to say that four times in five, under-garments are put on in a state of semi-dampness. What a fearful danger is here. We do not hesitate to say that every time a person changes his linen he does it at his peril.

This is such an age of bustle that comparatively few persons take time to digest their food. They swallow it, and run. Yet they complain of not being in good health. The wonder rather is that they do not fall dead in the street, as, indeed, many of them do.

How often have doctors been called in to patients whom they find crouching by the fireside and complaining of indigestion? Too many medical men pamper such patients, though it is their plain duty to tell the truth. And what is the truth? Why, simply this, that after dinner the patient is in the habit of spending his evening in an arm-chair, when he ought to be out in the open air, walking off the effects of his heavy meal.

Those who work hard ought to eat plentifully, or they will find that they are burning the candle at both ends. Surely no science is required to prove this. Work is, so to speak, a furnace, and the brighter the fire the more coals it ought to be fed with, or it will go out. Yet we are a people who let our systems go down by disregarding this most elementary and obvious rule of health.

If doctors could afford to be outspoken they would, twenty times a day, tell patients that they are simply suffering from over-eating themselves. Every foreigner who visits this country is struck by this propensity of ours to eat too much.

Very heart-breaking are the statistics now to hand from America about the increase in smoking. That this fatal habit is also growing in favor in this country, every man who uses his eyes must see. What will be the end of it we shudder to think, but we warn those in high places that if tobacco smoking is not checked, it will sap the very vitals of this country.

Why is it that nearly every young man one meets in the streets is haggard and pale ? No one will deny that it is due to tobacco. As for the miserable wretch himself, his troubles will soon be over.

We have felt it our duty from time to time to protest against what is known as the anti-tobacco campaign. We are, we believe, under the mark in saying that nine doctors in every ten smoke, which is sufficient disproof of the absurd theory that the medical profession, as a whole, are against smoking. As a disinfectant, we are aware that tobacco has saved many lives. In these days of wear and tear, it is especially useful as a sedative ; indeed, many times a day, as we pass pale young men in the streets, whose pallor is obviously due to over-excitement about their businesses, we have thought of stopping them, and ordering a pipe as the medicine they chiefly require.

Even were it not a destroyer of health, smoking could be condemned for the good and sufficient reason that it makes man selfish. It takes away from his interest in conversation, gives him a liking for solitude, and deprives the family circle of his presence.

Not only is smoking excellent for the health, but it makes the smoker a better man. It ties him down more to the domestic circle, and loosens his tongue. In short, it makes him less selfish.

No one will deny that smoking and drinking go together. The one provokes a taste for the other, and many a man who has died a drunkard had tobacco to thank for giving him the taste for drink.

Every one is aware that heavy smokers are seldom heavy drinkers. When asked, as we often are, for a cure for the drink madness, we have never any hesitation in advising the application of tobacco in larger quantities

Finally, smoking stupefies the intellect.

In conclusion, we would remind our readers that our deepest thinkers have almost invariably been heavy smokers. Some of them have gone so far as to say that they owe their intellects to their pipes.

The clerical profession is so poorly paid that we would not advise any parent to send his son into it. Poverty means insufficiency in many ways, and that means physical disease.

Not only is the medical profession overstocked (like all the others), but medical work is terribly trying to the constitution. Doctors are a short-lived race.

The law is such a sedentary calling, that parents who care for their sons' health should advise them against it.

Most literary people die of starvation.

Trades are very trying to the young ; indeed, every one of them has its dangers. Painters die from blood poisoning, for instance, and masons from the inclemency of the weather. The commercial life on 'Change is so exciting that for a man without a specially strong heart to venture into it is to court death.

There is, perhaps, no such enemy to health as want of occupation. We would entreat all young men, therefore, whether of private means or not, to attach themselves to some healthy calling.

SHUTTING A MAP.

PROMINENT among the curses of civilization is the map that folds up " convenient for the pocket." There are men who can do almost everything except shut a map. It is calculated that the energy wasted yearly in denouncing these maps to their face would build the Eiffel Tower in thirteen weeks.

Almost every house has a map warranted to shut easily, which the whole family, working together, is unable to fold. It is generally concealed at the back of a press, with a heavy book on it to keep it down. If you remove the book, the map springs up like a concertina. Sometimes after the press is shut you observe something hanging out. This is sure to be part of the map. If you push this part in, another part takes its place. No press is large enough to hold a map that shuts. This is because maps that shut are maps that won't shut. They have about as much intention of shutting when you buy them as the lady has of obeying her husband when she gives a promise to that effect in the marriage service.

Maps that shut may also be compared to the toys that whistle, spin, or jump when the shopman is showing you how to work them, or to the machinery that makes mangling a pleasure, or to the instrument that sharpens a pencil in no time. These are completely under the control of the shopman, but after you have bought them and taken them home they become as uncertain in temper as a nervous dog.

The impossibility of shutting maps except by accident having been long notorious, it is perhaps remarkable that the public should go on buying them. There are hundreds of persons engaged at this moment upon making maps that shut (as the advertisement puts it), and there must, therefore, be a demand to meet such a supply. It is vanity that brings so many people to folly.

To do the nineteenth century justice, no one nowadays enters a shop with the object of buying a map that shuts. Wives, especially young ones, have asked their husbands to buy curious things for them; and husbands, especially old ones, have done it without being asked. But no wife who ever valued her domestic happiness has ever requested her husband to run into a shop in passing and buy a map that shuts. Even if she did, the husband would refuse. He might buy "Pigs in clover" if she wanted it; but the map puzzle, never.

Yet it has to be sorrowfully admitted that the street could be paved with the maps we do buy. Vanity is the true cause of our fall, but a shopman is the instrument. That even shopmen can shut maps which do not shut except in the shop, no thoughtful person believes; but over a counter they do it as easily and prettily as a conjurer plays with cards.

"Have you seen this new map?" they ask with affected carelessness, while they tie up your books.

"Anything special about it?" you reply, guardedly.

"Well, yes; it is very convenient for the pocket."

At the words "convenient for the pocket"

14

you ought to up with your books and run, for they are a danger signal; but you hesitate and are lost.

"You see," he goes on, "it folds into unusually small space."

This is merely another way of saying, "You see this is the worst kind of map that has been yet invented."

"These maps that shut are so difficult to shut," you venture to say. He laughs.

"My dear sir," he says, "a child could shut this one."

Then he opens and shuts it like a lady manipulating her fan, and a fierce desire grows within you to do likewise. When you leave the shop you take away with you a map convenient for the pocket.

What makes you buy it? In your heart you know that you are only taking home a pocketful of unhappiness, but you have the pride of life. 'In an age when we have made slaves of electricity and steam, it seems humiliating that we cannot shut a map. We have ceased, as a people, to look for the secret of perpetual motion, but we still hanker after the secret of how to shut a map.

No doubt the most maddening thing about maps that shut is that they do shut occasionally. They never shut, however, when you are particularly anxious that they should do so—before company, for instance. Very probably you take the map with you from the shop to your office, and there open it up. To your delight it shuts quite easily. This gives you a false feeling of security. If you would really know whether this map shuts more easily than the various other ones over which you have lost your temper, ask your office-boy to come in and see you shut it. You will find that it no longer shuts. This is a sure test.

Instead of experimenting in this way, and ordering the boy out of the room when you see him trying to get his face behind his hand, you are so foolish as to take the map home with you, to let your wife see how easily it shuts. If you are a keen observer you will notice her turn white when she sees you produce the map from your pocket. She knows there will be no harmony this evening, and her first determination is to keep the map from you until after dinner.

What follows when you produce the map and

begin, is too well known to require description.
What you ought to do in the circumstances no
one out of a pulpit could tell you, but there
are certain negative rules which it would be
well if you would observe.   For instance—

Do not be too sanguine.—Your tendency is
to open the map with a flourish, as one sometimes unfurls a handkerchief. Accompanied
by the remark that nothing is easier than to
shut a map once you have the knack of it, this
raises hopes which are not likely to be realized.
The smile of anticipatory triumph on your face
loses you the sympathy which is your right at
such a moment.   If you are over-confident, the
feeling is that your failure will do you good.
On the other hand,

Keep your misgivings to yourself.—Most
men, however confident they have been when
thinking of the ease with which they can close
maps, lose hope at the last moment, and admit
that perhaps they have forgotten the way.   This
is a mistake, for there is always just a possibility
of the map's shutting as easily as an ordinary
book.   Should you have prefaced your attempt
with misgivings, you will not get the credit of
this, and it will be ascribed to chance. There-

fore, be neither too sanguine nor too openly doubtful.

Don't repeat the experiment.—This, of course, is in the improbable event of your succeeding the first time. At once hand over the map to your wife, as if you had solved the puzzle forever. Encouraged by your success she will probably attempt it also and fail, when the chances are that she will ask you to do it again. As you value her good opinion of you, decline to do so. Make any excuse you think best. To carry out the description more completely, lie back in your chair, and smile good-naturedly at her futile efforts. Put on the expression of being amused at seeing her unable to do so simple a thing. As a result she will think more of you than ever—if possible.

Don't boast.—The chances, of course, are that you will have no occasion to boast; but in the event of your succeeding by accident, don't wave your arms in the air, or go shouting all over the house, "I've done it, I've done it!" If you behave in this way your elation will undo you, and no one will believe that you can do it again. Control yourself until you are alone.

Don't speak to the map.—Now we come to the rules which should be observed if you fail. As the chances are forty-nine to one that you will fail, these rules are more important than the others. When you have got the map half folded, you will see that there is something wrong. Do not frown at this point, and say, "Confound you, what is the matter with you now?" The map will not answer. It will give you no assistance. You ought at once to realize that you and it have entered upon a desperate struggle.

Don't be rude.—You would like to shake it as a terrier shakes a rat; but forbear. You may remember that when you witnessed the illegal contest between Jem Smith and Kilrain they shook hands before trying to kill each other. In the same way you should look as if you had no ill-will toward the map, even when it is getting the better of you.

Don't fold it the wrong way.—When you can't discover the right way, don't clench your teeth and fold it by brute force. In this way you can no doubt appear to gain a momentary advantage over it, but your triumph is short-lived. The instant you take your hand off it,

the map springs up, and now, instead of finding it convenient for the pocket, you would
have some difficulty in packing it away in a
sack.

Don't put your fist through it.—When you
find that it will neither go this way nor that,
don't pummel it. Spread it out, and begin
again.

Don't tear it.—It is a waste of energy on
your part to do this, for it is sure to tear itself.
It can be relied upon for this alone.

Don't kick it round the room.—Though this
is a pleasure for the moment, it is not lasting.
When you come to yourself you see that the
proceeding has been undignified, and, besides,
the map is no nearer being folded than ever.
You cannot remember too persistently that a
map is not to be folded by bullying. On the
other hand, you can try kindness if you like.

*Don't deceive yourself into thinking you
have done it.*—Your wife has been wringing
her hands in anguish all the time you have
been at it, and is wildly anxious to get you off
to bed. It is now midnight. Accordingly,
should you double the map up, as if you were
making a snowball of it, she will pretend to

think that you have folded it. Don't be
deceived by her. However great the temptation to accept her verdict, remember that you
are a man, and have consequently a mind of
your own. Have the courage to admit defeat.

Don't blame your wife.—It is unmanly to
remark pointedly that you did it quite easily
when she was not by. To imply that she is in
league with the map against you is unworthy
of a reasoning animal.

Don't lie.—In other words, if she leaves the
room for a moment, don't say you did it while
she was out.

Don't strike your boy.—The boy may snatch
it from your hands, and fold it in a moment.
There is great provocation in this, but don't
yield to it.

Don't take gloomy views of life.—Your
ignominious failure casts a gloom over the
household. Fling it off. Don't speak of your
expenditure being beyond your income, or of
having to sell the piano. Be cheerful; remember that there is nobler work for you to do
than that on which you have squandered an
evening, and that nobody can fold maps.

AN INVALID IN LODGINGS.

A TRUE STORY.

UNTIL my system collapsed, and my atten-
uated form and white face made me an object
for looking at, my landlady only spoke of me
as her parlor. At intervals I had communi-
cated with her through the medium of Sarah
Ann, the servant, when she presented her compliments (on a dirty piece of paper), and, as her
rent was due on Wednesday, could I pay my
bill now? Except for these monetary trans-
actions, my landlady and I were total strangers,
and, though I sometimes fell over her children
in the lobby, that led to no intimacy. Even
Sarah Ann never opened her mouth to me.
She brought in my tea, and left me to discover
that it was there. My first day in lodgings I
said " Good-morning " to Sarah Ann, and she
replied, " Eh?" " Good-morning," I repeated,

to which she answered contemptuously, " Oh,
ay." For six months I was simply the parlor,
but then I fell ill, and at once became an in-
teresting person.

Sarah Ann found me shivering on the sofa
one hot day a week or more ago, beneath my
rug, two coats, and some other articles. Then
I ate no dinner, then I drank no tea, and then
Sarah Ann mentioned the matter to her mistress. My landlady sent up some beef-tea, in
which she has a faith that is pathetic, and then
to complete the cure she appeared in person.
She has proved a nice, motherly old lady, but
not cheerful company.

"Where do you feel it worst, sir?" she
asked.

I said it was bad all over, but worst in my
head.

" On your brow?"

"No, on the back of my head."

" It feels like a lump of lead?"

" No, like a furnace."

" That's just what I feared," she said. " It
began so with him."

" With whom?"

" My husband. He came in one day, five

years ago, complaining of his head, and in three days he was a corpse."

"What?"

"Don't be afraid, sir. Maybe it isn't the same thing."

"Of course it isn't. Your husband, according to the story you told me when I took these rooms, died of fever."

"Yes, but the fever began just in this way. It carried him off in no time. You had better see a doctor, sir. Doctor was no use in my husband's case, but it is a satisfaction to have him."

Here Sarah Ann, who had been listening with mouth and eyes wide open, suddenly burst into tears, and was led out of the room, exclaiming, "Him sech a quiet gentleman, and he never flung nothing at me." Now, for the first time, did I discover that I had touched Sarah Ann's heart.

Though I knew that I had only caught a nasty cold, a conviction in which the doctor confirmed me, my landlady stood out for its being just such another case as her husband's, and regaled me for hours with reminiscences of his rapid decline. If I was a little better one day,

alas! he had been a little better the day before
he died, and if I answered her peevishly she told
Sarah Ann that my voice was going. She
brought the beef-tea up with her own hand,
her countenance saying that I might as well
have it, though it could not save me. Sometimes I pushed it away untasted (how I loathe
beef-tea now!), when she whispered something
to Sarah Ann that sent that tender-hearted
maid howling once more from the room.

" He's supped it all," Sarah Ann said, one
day, brightening.

"That's a worse sign," said her mistress,
" than if he hadn't took none."

I lay on a sofa, pulled close to the fire, and
when the doctor came my landlady was always
at his heels, Sarah Ann's dismal face showing
at the door. The doctor is a personal friend
of my own, and each day he said I was improving a little.

" Ah, doctor!" my landlady said, reprov-
ingly.

" He does it for the best," she explained to
me, " but I don't hold with doctors as deceive
their patients. Why don't he speak out the
truth like a man? My husband were told

the worst, and so he had time to reconcile himself.'

On one of these occasions I summoned up
sufficient energy to send her out of the room ;
but that only made matters worse.

" Poor gentleman ! " I heard her say to Sarah
Ann ; " he is very violent to-day. I saw he
were worse the moment I clapped eyes on
him. Sarah Ann, I shouldn't wonder though
we had to hold him down yet."

About an hour afterwards, she came in to
ask me if I " had come more round to myself,"
and when I merely turned round on the sofa
for reply, she said, in a loud whisper to Sarah
Ann, that I " were as quiet as a lamb now."
Then she stroked me and went away.

So attentive was my landlady that she was a
ministering angel. Yet I lay on that sofa plot-
ting how to get her out of the room. The
plan that seemed the simplest was to pretend
sleep, but it was not easily carried out. Not
getting any answer from me, she would ap-
proach on tiptoe and lean over the sofa, listening to hear me breathe. Convinced that I was
still living, she and Sarah Ann began a conversation in whispers, of which I or the deceased hus-

band was the subject. The husband had slept
a good deal, too, and it wasn't a healthy sign.

"It isn't a good sign," whispered my landlady, "though them as know no better might
think it is. It shows he's getting weaker.
When they takes to sleeping in the daytime
it's only because they don't have the strength
to keep awake."

"Oh, missus!" Sarah Ann would say.

"Better face facts, Sarah Ann," replies my
landlady

In the end I had generally to sit up and
confess that I heard what they were saying.
My landlady evidently thought this another
bad sign.

I discovered that my landlady held recep-
tions in another room, where visitors came who
referred to me as her "trial." When she
thought me distinctly worse, she put on her
bonnet and went out to disseminate the sad
news. It was on one of these occasions that
Sarah Ann, who had been left in charge of the
children, came to me with a serious request.

"Them children," she said, "want awful to
see you, and I sort of promised to bring 'em in,
if so you didn't mind."

"But, Sarah Ann, they have seen me often, and, though I'm a good deal better, I don't feel equal to speaking to them."

Sarah Ann smiled pityingly when I said I felt better, but she assured me the children only wanted to look at me. I refused her petition, but, on my ultimatum being announced to them, they set up such a roar that, to quiet them, I called them in.

They came one at a time. Sophia, the eldest, came first. She looked at me very solemnly, and then said bravely that if I liked she would kiss me. As she had a piece of flannel tied round her face, and was swollen in the left cheek, I declined this honor, and she went off much relieved. Next came Tommy, who sent up a shriek as his eyes fell on me, and had to be carried off by Sarah Ann. Johnny was bolder and franker, but addressed all his remarks to Sarah Ann. First, he wanted to know if he could touch me, and, being told he could, he felt my face all over. Then, he wanted to see the "spouter." The "spouter" was a spray through which Sarah Ann blew coolness on my head, and Johnny had heard of it with interest. He refused to leave the room until he had been permitted to saturate me and my cushion.

I am so much better now that even my land-lady knows I am not dying. I suppose she is glad that it is so, but at the same time she resents it. She has given up coming to my room, which shows that I have wounded her feelings, and I notice that the beef-tea is no longer so well made. The last time I spoke to her it was I who introduced the subject of her husband, and she spoke of him with a diminution of interest. His was a real illness, she said, with emphasis on the adjective that made me feel I had been drinking beef-tea on false pretenses.

The children are more openly annoyed. In the innocence of youth they had looked upon me as a sure thing, and had been so "good" for nearly a week that they feel they will never be able to make the lost time up. I understand that their mother had to break my recovery to them gently.

But Sarah Ann's is the severest blow. For years, Sarah Ann has been a servant in lodging-houses, with nobody and nothing to take any interest in. She has seen many lodgers come and go without knowing who or what they were, and she has never had a mistress who thought her of any importance. In these circumstances the neglected one takes, in story-books, to tending a flower in a broken pot, for which she conceives a romantic attachment. The devotion Sarah Ann might have given to a tulip she bestowed on me. For a week I believed she loved me, but only on the understanding that I was leaving this world behind me. Her interest in me was morbid, but sincere. I was the only thing she had ever been given to look after. If I had gone the way of my landlady's husband, I am confident that Sarah Ann would have remembered me for the whole summer. But it was not to be, and she has not enough spirit to complain. When she comes in to remove the breakfast things and finds that I have eaten two eggs and four slices of toast she says nothing, but I hear her sigh. In the over-mantel I see her looking at me so reproachfully that I have not the heart to be angry with her. If Sarah Ann's feelings could be analyzed it would be found, I believe, that she looks upon herself as a hopelessly unlucky person doomed to eternal disappointments. In another week's time I expect to be able to go

15

to my office as usual, when Sarah Ann and I will again be strangers. Already the children have given up opening my door and peeping in. There is an impression in the house that I am a fraud. They call me by my name as yet, but soon again I will be the parlor.

THE MYSTERY OF TIME-TABLES.

THE history of the time-table is probably this. When the first one was issued, travelers accepted it in the spirit in which it was produced: as an amusing puzzle with no solution. By and by they began to tire of the puzzle, and then a clever advertisement (in the form of a paragraph) appeared in the papers declaring that a gentleman (" whose name and address we are not at liberty to mention") had solved the puzzle, and discovered that time-tables really told you when your train started. This revived interest in the subject; several persons wrote to the *Times*, maintaining that time-tables were for use as well as ornament, and, to be brief, a cry arose that there was more in time-tables than met the eye. One man, who only traveled between London and Bristol, while admitting that the time-table was upside down as to that line, held that if he traveled between Manchester and Newcastle he could look up the trains quite easily; a second found that his time-table told him when his train started for Manchester, only it always turned out to be a Sunday train; and a third declared that the time-table would enable him to catch the train for Scotland were it not for alterations made in the beginning of the month. Soon time-tables were as much a subject of controversy as Ibsen is to-day. There were the Tableites, as they were called, just as we have the Ibsenites. The Tableites were the out-and-out believers in time-tables, the persons who found a profound meaning in every figure. At first they were few in number, while the Anti-Tableites were many; but the minority were enthusiastic over their discovery, and made a creed of it. They wrote plays and novels in which Tableites married and found the missing will, while the Anti-Tableites were left to die at Waterloo Station, looking vainly for the way out. Of course, the Anti-Tableites retorted, going so far as to say that time-tables are immoral; but the great general public is ever greedy of a new thing, and soon Tableism was the fashion. At the present moment there is hardly a man or woman in the United Kingdom who would dare to say that he or she knows time-tables to be frauds. Yet in what is called our innermost heart we are all aware that time-tables remain a puzzle, and that we only carry them about with us and look knowingly at them because it is the national form of swaggering. No one can really look up his train in a time-table.

Then how (the African monarch who is to be the next season's lion might ask) do the great English-speaking people catch their trains, for they certainly do travel a good deal? You, O reader, could answer that question. What is your procedure when you have decided to take a railway journey? It is this. You say to your wife, quite solemnly, that she had better send out for a new time-table. She says, with equal solemnity, that there is a time-table somewhere; and you reply that you must have a new one, as there are sure to be alterations this month. Then you slip out of the house and proceed to St. Pancras, where you bribe or threaten a porter into telling you when your train starts. Returning home, you find the

new time-table lying ready for you, and, as
soon as your wife enters, you open it and mutter:
" Hem! Ha! Very awkward! Just so!   Have
I time to catch the connection at Normanton ?
Let me see whether the Great Northern would
not suit better," and so on.   Finally you say
you see that the best train starts at a certain
hour.

Do you believe you have deceived your wife ?
Probably you think there is just a chance of
her having been taken in.   As a matter of fact,
she is aware that time-tables are as much a
mystery to you as to her, and she knows quite
well that you were at St. Pancras an hour ago.
But she keeps up the deception.   When she
married you she knew what men are, and that
on the subject of time-tables there must be
deceit between man and wife if they are to be
happy.   The ideal couple keep nothing from
each other, save this affair of the time-table, and
a wise wife, instead of asking her husband why
he occasionally looks as if he had a secret on
his mind, will understand that he is only feeling guilty of pretending to understand, " See
Willesden Junction K * 2 for Wednesday and
Saturday."   The perfect bride undertakes at

the altar to love, honor, and obey her husband, and pretend to believe that he can look up his train.

But all wives are not perfect, and one often hears it said of Mr. and Mrs. Such-a-One that they don't get on together. The name usually given to their complaint is incompatibility of temper, but inquiry, which we have no right to make, would prove four times in five that the wife has been so ill-advised as to challenge her husband's knowledge of time-tables. Men who will endure a great deal from their wives, and go on reading their paper at breakfast quite placidly, fire up at this. It is the one charge they cannot brook; it takes six inches from the height of a six-footer, and there will be no more happiness in that household until the wife apologizes with tears. A little experience will show her that nothing is to be gained by holding up her husband's one weakness to the light, and much by pretending that his skill in reading time-tables is a constant marvel to her. Speak of this skill in company when he is present, and there is nothing your husband will deny you. Politicians call each other everything that is bad, and yet one hears

now and again that they continue to dine together. The cynical say that this is because
politics deadens the conscience, and that seems
as good a reason as another. But not even
members of Parliament are absolutely hardened.
It is notorious that a few of them are not on
speaking terms, and that they quarreled over
time-tables. " The honorable gentleman is a
moral cut-throat, and that is the only moral
thing about him." " The honorable and gallant
member for Shillelagh is a poltroon," are merely
Parliamentary expressions; but tell a member
out of the House that he cannot look up his
train in a time-table, and he and you are enemies
forever. You cannot bring such a charge
against him in the House without being sent to
the Clock Tower.

These are all well-known facts, familiar to
every reader, but there is a conspiracy of
silence about them. Enter a railway compartment, and you find all your fellow-travelers
turning over the leaves of their time-table, with
the exception, perhaps, of one who has opened
his map and is making desperate efforts to
close it. You open your time-table, too; but,
instead of pretending to understand it, please

look over it at these other humbugs. The man in the corner, who has already asked six porters if this is the train for Doncaster, and is still doubtful, sees your eye on him, and says aloud, " Ha ! I see we reach Doncaster at 5 : 30." The man who is resting his feet on your Gladstone bag ostentatiously turns down a corner of his time-table to imply that he has found the page. The third man is boldly pretending that he finds the index a help. And so it goes on, and we all do it, and we are a nation of hypocrites, for not one of us can solve the riddle of the time-tables or find out anything from them, save that all the trains are running in the wrong direction. But why not be open, and admit that the time-tables are a mystery still ?

MENDING THE CLOCK.

IT is a little American clock, which I got as a present about two years ago. The donor told me it cost half-a-guinea, but on inquiry at the shop where it was bought (this is what I always do when I get a present), I learned that the real price was four-and-sixpence. Up to this time I had been hesitating about buying a stand for it, but after that I determined not to do so. Since I got it, it has stood on my study mantel-piece, except once or twice at first, when its loud tick compelled me to wrap it up in flannel, and bury it in the bottom of the drawer. Until a fortnight ago my clock went beautifully, and I have a feeling that had we treated it a little less hardly it would have continued to go well. One night a fortnight ago it stopped, as if under the impression that I had forgotten to wind it up. I wound it up as far as was possible, but after going for an hour it stopped again. Then I shook it, and it went for five minutes. I strode into another room to ask who had been meddling with my clock, but no one had touched it. When I came back it was going again, but as soon as I sat down it stopped. I shook my fist at it, which terrified it into going for half a minute, and then it went creak, creak, like a clock in pain. The last thing it did before stopping finally was to strike nineteen.

For two days I left my clock serenely alone, nor would I ever have annoyed myself with the thing had it not been for my visitors. I have a soul above mechanics, but when these visitors saw that my clock had stopped they expressed surprise at my not mending it. How different, I must be, they said, from my brother, who had a passion for making himself generally useful. If the clock had been his he would have had it to pieces and put it right within the hour. I pointed out that my mind was so full of weightier matters that I could not descend to clocks, but they had not the brains to see that what prevented my mending the clock was not incapacity, but want of desire to do so. This has ever been the worry of my life, that, because I don't do certain things, people take it for granted that I can't do them. I took no prizes at school or college, but you entirely misunderstand me if you think that that was because I could not take them. The fact is, that I had always a contempt for prizes and prizemen, and I have ever been one of the men who gather statistics to prove that it is the boy who sat at the foot of his class that makes his name in after life. I was that boy, and though I have not made my mark in life as yet, I could have done it had I wanted to do so as easily as I could mend a clock. My visitors, judging me by themselves, could not follow this argument, though I have given expression to it in their presence many times, and they were so ridiculous as to say it was a pity that my brother did not happen to be at home.

" Why, what do I need him for ? " I asked, irritably.

" To mend the clock," they replied, and all the answer I made to them was that if I wanted the clock mended I would mend it myself.

" But you don't know the way," they said.

" Do you really think," I asked them, " that

I am the kind of man to be beaten by a little American clock?"

They replied that that was their belief, at which I coldly changed the subject.

"Are you really going to attempt it?" they asked, as they departed.

"Not I," I said; "I have other things to do."

Nevertheless the way they flung my brother at me annoyed me, and I returned straight from the door to the study to mend the clock. It amused me to picture their chagrin when they dropped in the next night and found my clock going beautifully. "Who mended it?" I fancied them asking, and I could not help practicing the careless reply, "Oh, I did it myself." Then I took the clock in my hands, and sat down to examine it.

The annoying thing, to begin with, was that there seemed to be no way in. The clock was practically hermetically sealed, for, though the back shook a little when I thumped it on my knee, I could see quite well that the back would not come off unless I broke the mainspring. I examined the clock carefully round and round, but to open the thing up was as impossible as to get into an egg without chipping the shell. I twisted and twirled it, but nothing would move. Then I raged at the idiots who made clocks that would not open. My mother came in about that time to ask me how I was getting on.

" Getting on with what ? " I asked.

" With the clock," she said.

" The clock," I growled, " is nothing to me," for it irritated me to hear her insinuating that I had been foiled.

" But I thought you were trying to mend it," she said.

" Not at all," I replied ; " I have something else to do."

" What a pity," she said, " that Andrew is not here."

Andrew is the brother they are always flinging at me.

" He could have done nothing," I retorted, " for the asses made this clock not to open."

"I'm sure it opens," my mother said.

"Why should you be sure?" I asked, fiercely.

" Because," she explained, " I never saw or heard of a clock that doesn't open."

" Then," I snarled, "you can both see and hear of it now"—and I pointed contemptuously at my clock.

She shook her head as she went out, and as
soon as the door shut I hit the clock with my
clenched fist (stunning my fourth finger). I
had a presentiment that my mother was right
about the clock's opening, and I feared that
she still labored under the delusion that I had
been trying to mend the exasperating thing.

On the following day we had a visit from my
friend Summer, and he had scarcely sat down
in my study when he jumped up, exclaiming,
" Hullo, is that the right time ? "

I said to him that the clock had stopped, and
he immediately took it on his knees. I looked
at him sideways, and saw at once that he was
the kind of man who knows about clocks.
After shaking it he asked me what was wrong.

" It needs cleaning," I said at a venture, for
if I had told him the whole story he might have
thought that I did not know how to mend a
clock.

" Then you have opened it and examined
the works ? " he asked, and not to disappoint
him, I said yes.

" If it needs cleaning, why did you not clean
it ? " was his next question.

I hate inquisitiveness in a man, but I replied

that I had not had time to clean it. He turned it round in his hands, and I knew what he was looking for before he said :

" I have never taken an American clock to pieces. Does it open in the ordinary way ? "

This took me somewhat aback, but Summer, being my guest, had to be answered.

" Well," I said, cautiously, " it does and it doesn't."

He looked at it again, and then held it out to me, saying : " You had better open it yourself, seeing that you know the way."

There was a clock in the next room, and such a silence was there in my study after that remark that I could distinctly hear it ticking.

" Curiously unsettled weather," I said.

" Very," he answered. " But let me see how you get at the works of the clock."

" The fact is," I said, " that I don't want this clock mended; it ticks so loudly that it disturbs me."

" Never mind," Summer said, " about that. I should like to have a look at its internals, and then we can stop it if you want to do so."

Summer talked in a light way, and I was by

16

no means certain whether, once it was set agoing, the clock could be stopped so easily as he thought, but he was evidently determined to get inside.

"It is a curious little clock," I said to him; "a sort of puzzle, indeed, and it took me ten minutes to discover how to open it myself. Suppose you try to find out the way?"

"All right," Summer said, and then he tried to remove the glass.

"The glass doesn't come off, does it?" he asked.

"I'm not going to tell you," I replied.

"Stop a bit," said Summer, speaking to himself; "is it the feet that screw out?"

It had never struck me to try the feet; but I said: "Find out for yourself."

I sat watching with more interest than he gave me credit for, and very soon he had both the feet out; then he unscrewed the ring at the top, and then the clock came to pieces.

"I've done it," said Summer.

"Yes," I said, "but you have been a long time about it."

He examined the clock with a practiced eye, and then—

" It doesn't seem to me," he said, " to be requiring cleaning."

A less cautious man than myself would have weakly yielded to the confidence of this assertion, and so have shown that he did not know about clocks.

" Oh, yes, it does," I said, in a decisive tone.

" Well," he said, " we had better clean it."

" I can't be bothered cleaning it," I replied, " but, if you like, you can clean it."

" Are they cleaned in the ordinary way, those American clocks? " he asked.

" Well," I said, " they are and they aren't."

" How should I clean it, then ? " he asked.

" Oh, in the ordinary way," I replied.

Summer proceeded to clean it by blowing at the wheels, and after a time he said, " We'll try it now."

He put it together again, and then wound it up, but it would not go.

" There is something else wrong with it," he said.

" We have not cleaned it properly," I explained.

" Clean it yourself," he replied, and flung out of the house.

After he had gone I took up the clock to
see how he had opened it, and to my surprise
it began to go. I laid it down triumphantly.
At last I had mended it. When Summer came
in an hour afterwards he exclaimed—

" Hullo, it's going."

" Yes," I said, " I put it to rights after you
went out."

" How did you do it ? " he asked.

" I cleaned it properly," I replied.

As I spoke I was leaning against the mantel-
piece, and I heard the clock beginning to make
curious sounds. I gave the mantel-piece a
shove with my elbow, and the clock went all
right again. Summer had not noticed. He
remained in the room for half-an-hour, and all
that time I dared not sit down. Had I not
gone on shaking the mantel-piece the clock
would have stopped at any moment. When
he went at last I fell thankfully into a chair,
and the clock had stopped before he was half
way down the stairs. I shook it and it went
for five minutes, and then stopped. I shook
it again, and it went for two minutes. I shook
it, and it went for half a minute. I shook it,
and it did not go at all.

The day was fine, and my study window stood open. In a passion I seized hold of that clock and flung it fiercely out into the garden. It struck against the trunk of a tree, and fell into a flower-bed. Then I stood at the window sneering at it, when suddenly I started. I have mentioned that it has a very loud tick. Surely I heard it ticking! I ran into the garden. The clock was going again! Concealing it beneath my coat I brought it back to the study, and since then it has gone beautifully. Everybody is delighted except Summer. who is naturally a little annoyed.

THE BIGGEST BOX IN THE WORLD.

THE largest ship the seas have ever seen was not, as is generally held, the *Great Eastern*. It was the vessel in which William the Conqueror came over to England, bringing the ancestors of so many people with him. One thinks of this enormous ship when looking about him for anything with which to compare Glengarry's box. As William's ship is to other ships, so is Glengarry's box to all other boxes.

Glengarry is a medical in his ninth year. He has a romantic notion that he could really study if he had the proper surroundings. He finds that the sharp corners of a square room are against concentration, and that long rooms are depressing, and round rooms too exhilarating. In quest of the room that would suit him he changes his lodgings every month or so, but though his cab, with a ton of luggage on the top of it, and bags falling off the seat, is now a familiar sight in most Edinburgh streets, Glengarry has never yet come upon a room that has proved a real help.

It will already be seen why Glengarry began to think by day and night of a big box. He did not want it to study in, but to hold his things in, as he passed from one temporary home to another. In nine years he had accumulated a great many suits of clothes, and these Glengarry had to drag after him from lodging to lodging. In his passionate desire to become a doctor he has now hundreds of note-books, most of them left him by men who have got round the examiners; and at the University, where such things are talked of with bated breath, he is reputed to have the only complete collection of cribs and keys in Edinburgh. His rooms are thus a favorite resort.

After Glengarry had packed all his belongings, as he fondly thought, he usually discovered that he had forgotten the six volumes in manuscript entitled "How to Get the Soft Side of Turner," or twelve pairs of boots, or three old coats, or something else, and then the straps had to be taken off his boxes again when the lid jumped up, exploding the contents in all directions. Thus the idea of a box sufficiently gigantic to hold everything took possession of Glengarry to such an extent that he could almost have passed an examination in it.

Rumors that the box had been contracted for were passed from mouth to mouth at the University three months ago. These were at first scouted, as big undertakings—the Channel Tunnel, for instance—usually are; but it was noticed that Glengarry often wore a preoccupied look now, and was absenting himself from his classes even more frequently than usual. When asked to stand for the Students' Council he said that he had something else in his eye at present. Some thought that he referred to a scheme for writing the answers to all possible medical questions on his shirt-sleeves, but he was really thinking of the box. It was by this time in course of construction, the plans being Glengarry's own.

At that time Glengarry was living in Frederick Street, at the top of the house. The room was of such remarkable construction that it could not be classified, and when he took it he thought he had got what he was after at last. Bitter disappointment awaited him, however, for the wind howled up there all day long, and he cannot study in wind. He was anxious, too, to try his new box as soon as possible, so he engaged another room in Cumberland Street, where there was said to be no wind.

The night before Glengarry was to leave Frederick Street he sat waiting for his box as impatiently as though it were a letter in an angular hand. By this time he would, on former occasions, have been damp with perspiration, caused by his efforts to get all his things into three small boxes and five Gladstone bags. He would have been sitting on the boxes in wild attempts to close them, finding after they were closed that a coat sleeve was sticking out, or that the bootjack had taken advantage of some moment when he had his back to it, to leap out of a bag and hide beneath the table. His feet would have been catching in waistcoats which he could have sworn were at the bottom of box 2, and he would have had a presentiment that he had forgotten to pack his "Guide to the Ways of Graiager Stewart." Even after the boxes were so full that the locks refused to

work, and the Gladstone bags were of new and
strange shapes, looking like animals whose bones
wanted to burst the skin, he would have had to
make up brown paper parcels, out of which
books, brushes, and photograph frames would
fall as he carried them down the stair. But
the box was coming, and Glengarry smoked,
and chuckled at the surprise he would give
his things directly.

Glengarry was in this pleasing frame of mind,
as exultant as if a message had come asking
him to cut off a magistrate's leg, when the bell
rang. He tried not to look proud, but listened
eagerly to make sure that his landlady had
gone to the door. His landlady finished her
supper and put her children to bed, and then
remembered that the bell had been ringing
for some time. Soon afterwards she informed
Glengarry that two men wanted to see him,
also that they were using language. Glengarry
waved his hand grandly, and told her to show
them in.

" I suppose you have brought the box ? "
Glengarry said.

They said they had, and they wanted to
know what they were to do with it.

" Bring it in here," said Glengarry.

" We can't get it up the stair."

" What? It can't be heavy with nothing in it."

" No, but it's too big. If you want it up here you'll have to widen the passage."

Glengarry's pipe went out at this, and he said falteringly that he would come down and have a look at the box. When he saw it in all its magnitude, the box staggered him.

" Perhaps it could be got into your room by the window," one of the men said; " but you would have to take the window out first."

" And you would need a crane," said the other man, " to lift it up."

Glengarry measured the passage, and saw that the leviathan box could never enter it.

" Can you leave the box here all night?" he asked.

" You would be run in if we did that," the men said.

There was, therefore, nothing for it but to bribe them to take the box away again.

" Bring it back early in the morning," Glengarry said, " before there is much traffic. It might frighten the horses."

" They would take it for a steam tram," said the men.

That night Glengarry stole into Cumberland Street with a string, and measured the passage that led to his new lodgings. The passage was wide enough to admit the box. On the following evening two other medicals, Smith (seventh year) and Flint (sixth year), called at Cumberland Street as a deputation from the medical faculty, who wanted to know about the box. They were shown into Glengarry's new abode, and Glengarry welcomed them nervously.

" It looks like a good room for working in," said Smith, who always thinks he could work in other people's rooms, " but where is the box ? "

" You don't mean to say that you don't see it ? " asked Glengarry.

Smith and Flint looked round the room, and their eyes rested on what they had taken for a monster cupboard.

" Is it in there ? " asked Flint.

" In there ! " cried Glengarry, indignantly ; " that is it."

" What ? "

" The box."

"I took it for a bedroom," said Flint.

"It is more like a cabmen's shelter," said Smith.

When the visitors had come to, they wanted to know how the box was brought from Frederick Street, but at first Glengarry refused to gratify their curiosity. He was in need of sympathy, however, and gradually they got the story out of him.

Though the box had arrived at Frederick Street early in the morning, a crowd soon gathered round it, owing to an absurd rumor that it was to be erected as a house for the band in Princes Street Gardens. Glengarry had to carry all his things down to the box, and pack it there, and then the story went out that it was a furniture van. When the boys realized that the "show," as they termed it, belonged to Glengarry, they studied him as he packed, and for a time their gaze was reverent. Becoming used to the idea, however, they took to jumping over the box (and into it when the owner was on his way up or downstairs); to show that they appreciated the magnitude of his labors they gave three ringing cheers every time he appeared with another load.

Glengarry in his excitement was so foolish as to think that the box could be conveyed to Cumberland Street on a cab, but the cabmen whom he hailed gave him a piece of their mind. At last a lorry was got, and the box was raised upon it by six men, amid loud applause from the boys, who insisted on following the lorry to Cumberland Street, sadly and solemnly, as if they were walking in a funeral procession. Men and boys joined the crowd, as the fame of the box spread, and when it arrived at its destination all Cumberland Street was in a commotion.

The box was got into the passage and there it stood.

" Turn it on its side," cried Glengarry, but it would not turn.

" Pull it back," was his next suggestion, but it would not pull back.

The six men sat down on the steps and wiped their brows, and the boys danced with honest glee. Lodgers going out found their way blocked by the box, and had to climb over it. A lady who had been leaving tracts had to go up the stairs again and sit in some kitchen for an hour.

The policeman came and said :

" Come, you know, this won't do," and then strolled away.

Glengarry's new landlady apologized to all the people on the stairs for having allowed Glengarry to have the back parlor. She also warned Glengarry that if the box was brought up it would probably kill the people below.

A man on the opposite side of the street opened his window and shouted directions.

" Break the lid or the door of the thing," he cried, " carry up its contents in your arms."

Unfortunately the box was lying on its lid, and so the suggestion was not practical. At last the six men disappeared and came back with an axe. With this, one made a way into the box, and the boys shouted gleefully once more as they heard the axe smashing Glengarry's pictures.

All forenoon Glengarry was carrying up armfuls of books, boots, and clothing, and then the box itself was carried up. Glengarry grudged the money he had to pay those six men until the bill for the box came in, when he saw that the men had been cheap in comparison.

The box and Glengarry are in Cumberland Street still. Glengarry would have tried new rooms long ago if he could have left the box behind him, but the landlady refuses to accept it. The room is utterly unsuitable for working in, Glengarry not being able to work where there is no wind, and, consequently, he does not mean to go in for his final this year. His friends have suggested that the box might prove useful at an exhibition, not as an exhibit, but as a stall. Another suggestion is that the Senatus could put the Brewster statue in it at the time of the rectorial election.

17

THE COMING DRAMATIST.

SHAKESPEARE has three plays on the London stage at present, and several companies in the " provinces," where Sheridan, too, is holding up his head. This is even better than Mr. Pettitt, and has set those who write about the theatre a-talking. The manager who produces Shakespearean pieces gets a certificate of character from the critics, and theatre-goers are given to understand that he is a public benefactor. He has " the best interests of the stage at heart," and you ought to clap your hands when you look at him. So they say, but it is only a manner of talking. The manager who invites the populace to see himself as Hamlet in reduced circumstances, or his wife in Lady Teazle's dresses, is usually a greater bore than the comic person with red nose for trade-mark, or the melodramatic hero in a prologue and five acts. Even

when Shakespeare is efficiently presented, there
is no reason why we should exult over the fact,
as if each of the players merited a medal for
doing the best for himself; nor need we at once
begin to argue that the prospects of the theatre
are brightening. The old playwrights are popular with actors because of reasons that are
quite creditable, but not specially inspiring.
It is pleasant to feel that you are looked upon
as some one to honor the moment you produce
a Shakespearean play, and " Fame " being what
the actor murmurs to himself as he walks along
the streets, he naturally likes to appear in the
parts that give him his best opportunity. Hamlet is his favorite character when he is his
own manager, because it is the longest part in
Shakespeare. Another weighty reason is that
you can play the old dramatists for nothing.
Thus, though one is always glad to see actors
ambitious of great parts, it is not necessary to
extol them otherwise than for their acting. Mr.
Irving has, no doubt, done more for the stage
than any other living man, but only in the way
of showing that Shakespeare in magnificent
upholstery need not spell bankruptcy. By far
the healthiest sign of the stage would be the

appearance of new playwrights of distinction, and Mr. Irving seems to have given up looking for them. Obviously they are hard to find, but the actor or manager who discovers even one will have done better for the stage than those who revise Shakespeare to the end of their days.

That we should have no living playwrights to speak of is assuredly remarkable, for the demand is great : the rewards are such as to dwarf the honors attainable by novelists, poets, or essayists, and the pecuniary remuneration for a single successful play means a bank account forever. Miss Gubbins, author of the famous novel *Her Fourth Husband*, produces a silly play at a *matinée*, and every prominent daily paper in the country has half a column about it next morning. Mr. Wigley adapts the latest Ambiguous Comic piece, and sells the rights for five or ten thousand pounds. After that he is interviewed whithersoever his triumphal progress takes him, and London correspondents telegraph to Australia that he sometimes wears a white waistcoat. In short, the newspaper editors, who know what they are about, think that theatrical intelligence must be given in full, though important books have to wait for notice until Parliament rises. Such interest in the drama ought to produce a dramatist, but we have none of parts to be compared with, say, our eight or ten leading novelists. Mr. Gilbert is a wit when he is set to music, but his latest effort, *Brantinghame Hall*, was dull and trivial, and only proved that a proper playwright is not necessarily a playwright proper. Mr. Pinero has always been unsuccessful when he was in the least ambitious, farce being what suits him best, and his " dramas " or " comedies " being ever a curious mixture of comedy, farce, and " serious interest." Mr. Grundy is a smaller Pinero, and the melodramatists are to be forgotten as soon as possible. We do not nowadays even have the secret of burlesque, for our burlesques burlesque nothing, and are only music-hall entertainments, in which many ladies are the scenery, while agile gentlemen play the fool at twenty or fifty pounds a week. At this moment London is looking forward to seeing a comedian from the music halls turning Lancelot into ridicule. A few comic songs from the vulgar palaces that are now so fashionable in London will probably make this latest " burlesque" run for hundreds of nights. In Edinburgh the interest Londoners have in their music halls is not easily realized, though it is one of the worst signs of the times. The other night there was a disturbance in a London music hall over a comic political song, and since then innumerable " leaders " have solemnly discussed the question of politics in places of amusement. As a matter of fact, actors know nothing about the questions of the day. Not one in fifty records his vote in a Parliamentary election. Their politics are that Mr. Gladstone is the G. O. M., and that Lord Randolph Churchill curls his mustache.

In speaking of the theater of to-day, nevertheless, a pessimistic tone is uncalled for. The stage has been swept of many of its objectionable features, and the standard of acting has been immeasurably raised. If we have no one theater where the performance is of such uniform excellence as at one famous Paris playhouse, we have more actors and actresses of intelligence than any other country in the world. When the dramatist appears, scores of companies will be found capable of acting his pieces satisfactorily. Nor do we fear that he would be unappreciated. Trash is often a success on the stage, thanks to the talent of one or two of the players ; but the average audience recognizes good work, and would rejoice to have the opportunity of commending it. All that is wanted is the dramatist. One would think that there are novelists now with us who could write plays that would be literary as well as effective. Some of them have tried and failed, but obviously because they did not set about it in the proper way. Plays and novels require quite different construction, but the story-writer who is dramatic could become sufficiently theatrical by serving a short apprenticeship to the stage. There are such prizes to pluck for those who can stand on tiptoe that the absence of an outstanding dramatist is as surprising as it is disappointing.

As they were my friends, I don't care to say how it came about that I had this strange and, I believe, unique experience. They considered it a practical joke, though it nearly unhinged my reason. Suffice it that last Wednesday, when I called on them at their new house, I was taken upstairs and shown into a large room with a pictorial wall-paper. There was a pop-gun on the table and a horse with three legs on the floor. In a moment it flashed through my mind that I must be in a nursery. I started back, and then, with a sinking at the heart, I heard the key turn in the lock. From the corner came a strange uncanny moan. Slowly I forced my head round and looked, and a lump rose in my throat, and I realized that I was alone with It.

I cannot say how long I stood there motionless. As soon as I came to myself I realized that my only chance was to keep quiet. I tried to think. The probability was that they were not far away, and if they heard nothing for a quarter of an hour or so, they might open the door and let me out. So I stood still, with my eyes riveted on the thing where It lay. It did not cry out again, and I hoped against hope that It had not seen me. As I became accustomed to the room I heard It breathing quite like a human being. This reassured me to some extent, for I saw that It must be asleep. The question was, Might not the sleep be disturbed at any moment, and in that case, what should I do? I remembered the story of the man who met a wild beast in the jungle and subjugated it by the power of the human eye. I thought I would try that. All the time I kept glaring at Its lair (for I could not distinguish itself), and the two things mixed themselves up in my mind till I thought I was trying the experiment at that moment. Next it struck me that perhaps the whole thing was a mistake. The servant had merely shown me into the wrong room. Yes; but why had the door been locked? After all, was I sure that it was

locked? I crept closer to the door, and with
my eyes still fixed on the corner, put my hand
gently—oh, so gently!—on the handle. Softly
I turned it round. I felt like a burglar. The
door would not open. Losing all self-control,
I shook it; and then again came that unnatural
cry. I stood as if turned to stone, still clutch-
ing the door-handle, lest it should squeak if I
let it go. Then I listened for the breathing.
In a few moments I heard it. Before it had
horrified me; now it was like sweet music, and
I resumed breathing myself. I kept close to
the wall, ready for anything; and then I had
a strange notion. As It was asleep, why should
I not creep forward and have a look at it? I
yielded to this impulse.

Of course I had often seen Them before, but
always with some responsible person present,
and never such a young one. I thought it
would be done up in clothes, but no, it lay
loose, and without much on. I saw its hands
and arms, and it had hair. It was sound
asleep to all appearances, but there was a
queer smile upon its face that I did not like.
It crossed my mind that It might be only
shamming, so I looked away and then turned

sharply round to catch it. The smile was still there, but It moved one of its hands in a suspicious way. The more I looked, the more uncomfortable did that smile make me. There was something saturnine about it, and it kept it up too long. I felt in my pocket hurriedly for my watch, in case It should wake; but, with my usual ill-luck, I had left it at the watchmaker's. If It had been older I should not have minded so much, for I would have kept on asking what its name was. But this was such a very young one that it could not even have a name yet. Presently I began to feel that It was lying too quietly. It is not Their nature to be quiet for any length of time, and, for aught I knew, this one might be ill. I believe I should have felt relieved if It had cried out again. After thinking it over for some time I touched It, to see if It would move. It drew up one leg and pushed out a hand. Then I bit my lips at my folly, for there was no saying what It might do next. I got behind the curtain, and watched it anxiously through a chink. Except that the smile became wickeder than ever, nothing happened. I was wondering whether I should not risk pinching It, so as to make it scream and bring somebody, when I heard an awful sound. Though I am only twenty, I have had considerable experience of life, and I can safely say that I never heard such a chuckle. It had wakened up and was laughing.

I gazed at It from behind the curtain : its eyes were wide open, and you could see quite well that it was reflecting what it ought to do next. As long as it did not come out I felt safe, for it could not see me. Something funny seemed to strike it, and it laughed heartily. After a time It tried to sit up. Fortunately its head was so heavy that it always lost its balance just as it seemed on the point of succeeding. When It saw that It could not rise, It reflected again, and then all of a sudden It put its fist into its mouth. I gazed in horror ; soon only the wrist was to be seen, and I saw that it would choke in another minute. Just for a second I thought that I would let It do as It liked. Then I cried out, " Don't do that ! " and came out from behind the curtain. Slowly It removed its fist, and there we were, looking at each other.

I retreated to the door, but it followed me

with its eyes. It had not had time to scream yet, and I glared at It to imply that I would stand no nonsense. But, difficult though this may be to believe, it didn't scream when It had the chance. It chuckled instead, and made signs to me to come nearer. This was even more alarming than my worst fears. I shook my head and then my fist at It, but It only laughed the more. In the end I got so fearful that I went down on my hands and knees, to get out of its sight. Then It began to scream. However, I did not get up. When they opened the door they say I was beneath the table, and no wonder. But I certainly was astonished to discover that I had only been alone with It for seven minutes.

THE END.

www.ingramcontent.com/pod-product-compliance
Lightning Source LLC
Chambersburg PA
CBHW020345030726
47496CB00007B/2002